Marianne Wallenber

Marianne Wallenberg

REWINDING THE TAPE

Read
Summer 2001)
well

Reread spring 2022)

Memoirs
of
Marianne Wallenberg

New Dialogue Press
Binghamton, New York
2000

Library of Congress Cataloging-in-Publication Data:

First Edition, April 2000
Second Edition, November 2000

Marianne Wallenberg,
> *Rewinding The Tape, Memoirs of Marianne Wallenberg*

1. Autobiography   2. Music   3. Judaica
4. Immigration   5. Violins   6. Thomas Mann

Cover Design – Shalahudin Kafrawi
Formatting – Etin Anwar
Cover Image – front: Marianne Wallenberg c. 1935
             back: The three sisters

ISBN 1-58684-007-X

Published by New Dialogue Press and distributed by Global Publications
State University of New York at Binghamton
Binghamton, New York, USA 13902-6000
Phone (607) 777-4495 or 6104; Fax: (607) 777-6132
E-mail: pmorewed@bingamton.edu

Dedicated to my children,

Katherine and James

"If music be the food of love, play on..."
    –   Duke Orsino

William Shakespeare's *Twelfth Night*

TABLE OF CONTENTS

PREFACE IX

LEOPOLD 1

FAMILY..7

JEWISH IDENTITY..17

GROWING UP 23

MUSICAL BEGINNINGS..33

MUSIC AND THE CONSERVATORY 43

PARIS..49

ITALY 61

LONDON 67

IMMIGRATION 71

MUSIC IN NEW YORK CITY 79

CAMP LENORE 87

TOURING...91

MARRIAGE 117

BINGHAMTON 123

THE SYMPHONY 135

VIOLINS 149

FINALE 155

ACKNOWLEDGEMENTS 159

APPENDICES 161

- *LETTERS FROM THOMAS MANN* 163

- *FAMILY ALBUM* 169

PREFACE

Sometimes I wish somebody would invent a clock that goes backwards, like the rewind button on a cassette player. That's what happens in old age - you rewind your life's tape.

At 86 I am very much aware of the fact that I've beaten the odds in life, and that it is time to put it all on paper as a way of organizing my memories. It is a good time to take stock. And perhaps my children and whoever reads these pages may find a few facts, a few adventures, which may surprise or amuse them.

Life is a never-ending process of learning. In childhood, it's the basics; all through adulthood, it's a succession of revelations; and in old age, it's the realization of what it's all about.

Chapter 1

LEOPOLD

If someone should ask me what was the most important thing I learned in school, I would not hesitate to tell of an experience I had in the third grade. I had just been transferred from a private school, where my class consisted of six children from similar backgrounds as mine, to the Volksschule that was divided into two identical halves for boys and girls, with an enrollment of 600 youngsters of varied backgrounds.

The school was in a gray building which looked like a prison and where elderly Fräuleins ruled with iron hands, and often with large wooden sticks. Only about ten children in my class, including me, were by an unwritten law exempt from corporal punishment. This, as well as other privileges, was obviously determined by our economic status. The poorer the children, the worse they fared with the teachers.

I accepted this preferential treatment with the unquestioning silence of a pet that knows what's good for it. Nevertheless, the rough treatment inflicted on those poorer children never ceased to fill me with terror and anxieties, and even followed me into my dreams.

The teachers called us all by our last names. I particularly remember one girl, who seemed about the poorest of the poor. Her surname was Leopold, and she always wore what appeared to be the same dirty rags. She looked and smelled unwashed, and her hair had to be periodically deloused. Her desk stood separate from all the others, and when we filed in or out of the classrooms in pairs, she walked alone.

A day rarely passed without the teacher's wrath descending upon her in one form or another. It usually started with the teacher's question:

"Leopold, did you do your homework?"

No answer.

"Show me your papers."

No move, no answer.

"Come here and take your punishment."

School was something of a nightmare to me in those days, and learning in this atmosphere of terror amounted to precious little. I was about halfway through that third grade year when one day my parents took my sisters and me to a country fair in nearby Tutzing. Since roller coasters and Ferris wheels always made me sick to my stomach, I concentrated on the shooting, fishing, and ball–throwing contests, which offered a range of modest to wonderful prizes. At one of the galleries I had my heart set on a large, pink–beribboned doll, but I only managed to win a mysteriously wrapped "consolation prize."

"What is it?" my sisters asked eagerly while I unwrapped the oblong package. "It's nothing," I said, fighting back some tears as I held up the strange, ungainly object: a large wooden comb. It was crude and ugly and I had no use for it. But somehow I associated its very ugliness with the unkempt Leopold, and so the next morning at school I gave it to her. "Here," I said and shoved the comb over to her desk without looking at her or waiting to see whether she wanted it. Then I promptly forgot about it.

It is hard to describe what I felt when I saw her the following day. Her hair, which had always been a dark tangled mess, hung in silken strands down to her shoulders, and for the first time I saw that it was honey brown. I stared at her, speechless, as her little face lit up in a smile that was shyly triumphant and seemed to say, "You see, it's that simple." The terrible, shocking truth was there — she did not even have a comb.

Suddenly in that one shattering moment I began to understand the utter cruelty, bitterness, and loneliness of poverty. She didn't even have a comb — and that was why she was messy and dirty and dumb.

I don't know whether I managed to say anything to her. I don't know whether I spoke to anyone about what had just happened. But I am sure now that at that very moment I learned something no school books could ever teach me. It was a revelation I carried with me all my life. My heart had grown heavy with a new feeling that was infinitely sad and sweet, a feeling one might call compassion.

Chapter 2

FAMILY

A story goes like this: Two psychiatrists are comparing notes on their earliest childhood memories. One talks about floating in warm liquid which led through a dark narrow tunnel, "Then suddenly a burst of light, and my scream filled my lungs with air!" The other says, "Mm, birth. That is pretty good but I think I can do better. I remember going to a picnic with my father and coming home with my mother."

When short-term memory diminishes with age, long past events emerge ever more vividly and confirm what Marcel Proust said in *A la re-*

cherche du temps perdu: "La réalité ne se forme que dans la mémoire" (Reality is formed only in memory).

My own long-term memory reaches back somewhere between the age of two and three. I was born just before World War I in Munich — beautiful then, and even more so now, rebuilt after it was bombed in the Second World War. My father Paul Lissmann was the only son of our loving grandparents, who were hard working people, prospering with a silk textiles store in a big building they owned in the center of town, near the Marienplatz. After accumulating a certain amount of wealth while still relatively young, they said, "Enough of work," sold the business, and did some traveling. Although extensive travel was not the norm in those days, they visited Egypt, and the picture they took there of my grandmother riding a camel will be forever etched on my mind.

I must have been around ten years old when my grandfather died of Parkinson's Disease after a long illness. I was not at first particularly affected, even though it was the first time that death struck in my family; but when I saw my father a little later, red–eyed and quiet, I was overcome. A grown–up, my father, crying. It was only then that I was touched and started to cry myself.

To his parents' great regret my father had opted not to take over their textile business, but instead became a doctor — a neurologist and general practitioner. Although the medical profession was then not as near the top of the financial scale as it is now, his practice flourished due to his sunny disposition, knowledge, and dedication, which made him very popular with his patients.

Father was also a Mason. He rarely spoke to us about this, but I knew that it was some kind of brotherhood. He sometimes spoke of a lodge "brother" and a lodge that Mozart had belonged to.

In 1927 my father, long before the damaging influence of excessive exposure to the sun was common knowledge, wrote a book called *Lerne Richtig Sonnenbaden* (Learn to Sunbathe Correctly). The dedication reads, "Gewidmet meinen Kindern, dem Sonnenschein meines Lebens" (To my children, the sunshine of my life). When the second edition of this little book appeared just before Christmas, 1928, my father immediately went out and bought a record player for us — a costly, much coveted present in those days. As he had no hobbies, his profession and his family consumed most of his time. He had a taste in music that leaned towards the lighter side, preferring, for instance, operetta to opera.

Being very patriotic, he volunteered his medical services to the Army in 1914. In the course of the war he was awarded the Iron Cross, equivalent to somewhere between the American Silver Star and Distinguished Service Cross. Had he but known what would become of his beloved Germany in 1933! No matter how little his Jewish religion had meant to him, I am convinced my father would have emigrated with all of us to America right then. Although my mother's sisters lived in England, he would never touch English soil because, he said, "England made us lose the war."

My mother was born Luise Dünkelsbühler in Nüremberg. I hardly knew my maternal grandparents since my mother was the "caboose" of her family, eighteen years younger than her oldest sister. Her interests were in the arts, mainly literature and music. She was a very talented amateur pianist, and would nowadays probably have taken up professional studies. But her foremost desire, as it was for almost all females her age, was to get married and have children.

Like many people in their generation, both my parents rode bicycles. I recall a story that once my mother was riding home after dark on her bike, without a lamp on it, and a policeman stopped her. He was ready to slap her with a fine, but when she gave her name he said, "Dr. Lissmann? Oh, I was his patient! Now just wait till I turn the corner and you can ride on. You won't meet another cop on your way to your home."

Already by 1925 my father had graduated from a bicycle to a motorcycle. When he had an accident on an unpaved country road and broke his leg, he decided to buy a Fiat, long before any of our friends owned a car. In 1929 at only the age of 50, Father died of a strep infection, an infection that nowadays could easily be cured with antibiotics. My poor grandmother, who on most Friday nights went to synagogue, stopped going because she was angry with God, whom she blamed for robbing her of both her children. (A daughter had died in the 1870s, during the diphtheria epidemic that had swept the United States and Western Europe). After my father's death my grandmother generously and immediately turned over her wealth to my mother, who was left with three teenage children and no income or money in savings, due to the runaway inflation of the early '20s (partly because of reparation payments extracted by the victors of World War I).

My childhood in Munich after World War I and during the period of German inflation was the relatively sheltered kind enjoyed by the Jewish upper middle class. We were a family of three girls, much to the chagrin of my father, who loved us, but like most fathers would have liked to have had a boy. My oldest sister Edith was lively, talkative, and ever ready to laugh. One day in school something funny went through her mind and she started to laugh. The teacher asked, "Edith, what's so funny?" Having forgotten what it was, she said, "I don't know," and then the whole class, including the teacher, started laughing.

Irene, three and a half years younger than I, was the clever one, a bit stubborn, and, as a child, quite amusing in her ways. One day at our round dinner table our parents were explaining to us some peoples' belief in reincarnation. Irene, still a tiny tot in her high chair, piped up, with an ascending scale on the final syllable: "Perhaps I once was a lion!"

Of Irene, Father only half–jokingly said, "This one should have been a boy." I wonder if people in those days were aware of psychological influences. Undoubtedly my father's statement had an effect on my little sister: She unconsciously tried to live up to the image of a boy — wearing her hair cut short like a boy, and being extremely sportive (she climbed the Matterhorn while still in her teens).

I was the typical middle child, squeezed, shy, and introverted. I blushed for no reason when people just looked at me, or even at the dinner table simply when I was spoken to. I was, however, our father's openly declared favorite, for the simple reason that I had blond hair, which I wore long, like everyone else. But in the mid-'20s, perhaps as the trend for women's emancipation grew, most women cut their hair short and the *Bubikopf* became the fashion. All of my classmates wore it, except me. I was not allowed to follow the trend because of my father's pronouncement that "you don't cut blond hair." To be the exception among a vast majority did not help my low self-esteem, and it was my mother with her fine psychological insight who intervened with my father. He gave in, but it nearly broke his heart when I brought my neatly ribboned ponytail to him.

Together with my sisters, I was brought up by two adoring parents who gave us a secure and warm family life. Profound ethics replaced any religion, and provided a strong emotional foundation. Even if the rules were relatively strict compared to upbringing nowadays, we felt so enveloped in our parents' love that saying the words "I love you," seemingly required by modern psychology, was not necessary.

At that time makeup for women was mainly used by the lower class and not generally accepted. I stated emphatically that "I cannot love a mother who uses makeup." I'll never forget the day I browsed around my mother's toiletries and discovered a small closed aluminum tube, the size of a short pencil. Rather shaken, I hesitated a long time, not daring to open it, dreading to see my worst fear confirmed. Yet I had to know — and found out that it was a brown eyebrow pencil. Good God, there was the dreadful proof. Closing it up, I stood still, expecting something terrible inside me to happen, like my love for my mother to fall into pieces. Yet nothing happened. And then quickly, immensely relieved, I walked away and soon forgot about it. Years later in a French class I took at the Sorbonne I wrote an essay on a theme that summed up my experience that day, "*Le coeur a ses raisons que la raison ne connaît point*" (The heart has its reasons which reason knows nothing of). Blaise Pascal's phrase is a theme that has resurfaced several times throughout my life.

Chapter 3

JEWISH IDENTITY

During my youth the general trend of the German Jews ran towards assimilation. We and our friends wanted to be first of all German — like everyone else — in order to escape age-old Jewish discrimination and centuries of persecution. So strong was the desire of my parents and all their friends to assimilate that they almost totally abandoned their Jewish identity and denied their religious inheritance. Judaism to me was a religion, a faith, not a racial heritage, and so I did not regard myself as being Jewish. My sisters and I were brought

up without any spiritual instruction: no prayers,
no worship. Instead, my parents relied entirely
on ethical guidelines; and it worked. We did
have a Bible geared for children with pretty illus-
trations of the stories of the Old Testament. The
pictures of Abraham and Isaac and Cain and
Abel fascinated me, and the concept of "God"
was ever present. But my father considered
himself a German above all else.

   We did not feel that we missed anything;
we had a Christmas tree like everybody else; and
presents were spread out on an enlarged dining
table, with a designated place for everybody, including the maids. For us, Christmas was a fes-
tivity without any religious significance. We
decorated a tree with live candles, opened presents, ate goose or carp and sang "O, Tan-
nenbaum." My grandfather, evidently a liberal–
minded man, came from his nearby residence to
join in the celebration — I think more as an
onlooker than a participant. But Grandmother,
more principled in her beliefs, stayed home, eat-

ing her heart out because she was missing it all. Her Jewish morals simply did not allow her to take part.

Did I say prayers? I think so — to a neutral God. But those prayers were intense wishes, such as, "Please let me wake up just two inches taller tomorrow morning." When we lined up in gym according to size, like the pipes on an organ, I was always at the tail end. This didn't hurt my popularity, though: My classmates gave me the good–natured (but to me embarrassing) pet name of Flöhle, or "Little flea."

When I was about ten I confided to my mother: "I want to become Catholic." Puzzled, she asked why. "Because Anni (the cook) said if I don't become Catholic I'll go to hell when I die." My mother wisely reassured me that I could wait with this decision until I was grown up, and then I could choose whatever religion I wanted. What a relief! And I'm sure Anni was told in no uncertain terms to stop proselytizing.

I suffered few insults of personal anti–Semitism in my early years. However, once on my way to school, on foot of course — as there were no school buses then — a classmate from the same neighborhood who often walked with me suddenly declared: "I'm not allowed to go with you any more because you crucified Jesus Christ." When I reported the incident to my parents, instead of offering a meaningful explanation they brushed over it, saying this was just utter nonsense, and to pay no more attention to her. I think my classmate was as nonplused as I was; yet for a while we still walked together. When we finally separated I was perplexed, but not too sorry about it as she was not a great friend of mine. Somewhat later I figured out what must have prompted her remark: her obviously anti–Semitic parents, the kind who would eventually help Hitler rise to power, might well have said, "Don't associate with Marianne Lissmann, Eleanor, because she is Jewish. Don't you know the Jews crucified Christ?"

Many years later, one of the most memorable trips I ever took was to Israel. I went alone as Fritz, my husband, was not a sight–seer and was willing to stay behind for those eleven days. I went with a tour group — there were only about twelve of us in a station wagon. The most overwhelming of all the sites we visited was Yad Vashem, a memorial to the six million. There, in a barely lit room on stone plates on the floor, were the names of all the concentration camps – – Dachau, Auschwitz, etc. I am still deeply moved when I think of it.

I always happened to look "Aryan" — blond, blue–eyed, fair–skinned, with an up-turned nose. (The hairdresser in America said I was a "shiksa," a new word to me, as my parents frowned upon using Yiddish words or gestures). My so-called "Aryan" looks, though, once had a disturbing effect on me. When I was a child the concept of adoption had been explained to us, although we knew of no adoptees among our friends or acquaintances. My older sister Edith was the spitting image of our mother, and people often remarked on this. "Irene," they would say, "is a Lissmann." "Marianne," they sounded puzzled, "doesn't look like anybody." These remarks, often repeated, gave rise to thoughts that maybe I *was* adopted. I knew and felt that I was loved and I was treated exactly like my sisters; but how was I ever going to find out? Far too inhibited, I never talked to anybody about this and gradually forgot about it, although some snide remarks by certain acquaintances putting my mother's fidelity in doubt didn't help. But I must admit that years later, when I obtained a copy of my birth certificate for immigration purposes, I felt a twinge of satisfaction.

Chapter 4

GROWING UP

Munich in the twenties was a good city in which to grow up. We lived close to the Englischen Garten, a beautiful park where we were taken almost daily for what is now called "exercise," but then meant "getting fresh air." The park had a slow-moving carousel and next to it a "Chinese Tower" — a five-tiered wooden construction in Chinese style whose first level had a band that played popular music. Little did I know in 1921 that the cellist in the band, a young engineering and music student from Danzig who supplemented his meager

earnings by this activity, would be my future
husband.

Our house in Munich, where I was born,
was made of stone and had a music room, living
and dining rooms, three bedrooms and one tiny
room for the maids. The kitchen was coal–fired
until we had gas. I loved looking into the fire,
but my father discouraged it because he didn't
want me to learn to love fire. We didn't mingle
with the neighbors, even though all the houses
were connected.

Those were lean years in Germany. Ram-
pant inflation melted everybody's savings to
zero. It was normal for my father to bring home
the money he had taken in from his medical patients by noon so that my mother could buy groceries in the afternoon before it lost half its value
by the next day. On one occasion Father gave
each of us three children one thousand German
Marks to spend at will. My sister Edith immediately went out and bought a notebook she had
long hankered for. I waited for one day and all I

could get for one Mark was a pencil. After two more days, one Mark bought nothing, but the store owner, feeling pity for my little sister, gave her a free piece of candy. Later on, I remember when the streetcar conductor had me get off four stops before my normal stop because I had only a fistful of Thousand-Mark bills, which didn't add up to the required fare.

In childhood you take for granted what life offers. My two sisters and I did not feel deprived when we drank cocoa made with water instead of milk. Eggs for supper were considered a feast; and a trolley car ride home with my mother to save the taxi fare after a tonsillectomy was accepted as how things had to be.

My first two school years were pleasant enough. They were spent at the private home of a middle–aged spinster where my schoolmates were four other girls and one boy. When we became unruly and noisy, Fräulein Laumen achieved order and silence by loudly tapping the table with her ruler. It came as a rude awaken-

ing when Fräulein Laumen retired and I had to
enter the Volksschule, as I related earlier in the
story of Leopold.

In the new school I envied some of the
girls who came to school barefoot — walking on
smooth city pavement felt so much nicer than
the prickly country roads we walked on when we
took off our shoes during vacations. Much later I
learned that these children went barefoot because their parents couldn't afford to buy them
shoes, or had to save them for the cold winters.

We spent our summer vacations at Egern
on Tegernsee in the German Alps, about a two-
hour train ride south from Munich. Adjoining
Egern at the lake was a lovely village with a narrow high–pointed church steeple typical of most
Bavarian villages. As soon as we were in the
country, the first thing we did was to take our
shoes off and go exploring. That's when I saw
and smelled "juicy" dung heaps, where I was
stung by bees, and where I saw chickens literally
running around without heads. One quite terri-

fying scene occurred in the shed of the farm-house we stayed at. I watched with horror as the farmer caught one of his chickens, lifted its upper body onto a large wooden block and with one swoop of an ax chopped off its head. He then dropped it to the ground, where the headless chicken ran around for several seconds before it collapsed and fell dead.

Not until I had moved to Binghamton, New York, did I come across similar country scenery. During our walks on the hills surrounding Binghamton we passed by the Gardner farm which had a real dung heap, three caged rabbits in the hay–filled shed, a large herd of sheep grazing in the sloping meadows, and cows being driven into their stables. The farm is gone now, though the vast view, beautiful in all directions, remains unaltered. I miss that spot where sights and smells linked me with my childhood.

At Tegernsee I also tried my hand at fishing. I was given a small fishing rod, nothing fancy, just a simple stick to which I attached a

plain string, plus a fishing hook, the only mone-
tary expenditure for the outfit. I dug up worms
for bait but became so nauseated piercing them
with the fishhook — their innards squishing out
— that I dumped the whole carefully gathered
potful into the lake. The fish must have had a
feast; and thus ended my fishing career.

One of the more pleasant summer activi-
ties in the country was berry picking — wild
raspberries, blueberries and the tiny strawberry
not much bigger than the size of a pea.
Strangely, the wild raspberries almost all had
worms inside, but we discovered a clever way to
get rid of them. By placing the berries into a
large bowl and draping a damp cloth over the
bowl overnight, we found that by morning all the
little worms had crawled up onto the cloth. That
way, we enjoyed the berries without their added
protein.

Next to the dock, where I had made my
feeble fishing attempts, was a crossboat station.
The Tegernsee is shaped like the figure eight,

only without the two loops touching in the middle. This gap was crossed for public transportation by a large heavy rowboat which, for fifteen pfennig a head, was paddled by a sturdy old man with a gray beard and a weather–beaten face. From my dock I watched him with fascination instead of paying attention to my fishing pole.

Across the road from the dock was the villa of the famous singer, Leo Slezak. His front garden was covered with phlox, all lilac and white, towering way above me. To this day, phlox has the sweet smell of childhood for me.

Our parents took us for hikes up the moderately high mountains, but it was an ordeal for me because I was not strong as a child. The exercise proved beneficial, though, and probably accounted for my love of hiking later on. Who knows whether I would have been able to carry my skis up the mountains in my later teens had I not been trained by these childhood hikes. Skiing became my one passionate sport. I also tried tennis, but because I was extremely near-sighted I always missed the ball and got thoroughly discouraged.

Before I was to begin my first year of school, I had a bout of pleurisy, and was sent to recuperate at a country home with six or seven other children. Healthy country food and country air were supposed to strengthen my frail body, but I don't think they helped very much because I was homesick all the time.

Among the children at the home was a little boy whose parents lived in Munich and owned a candy store, well–known to me. Every week he received a package from his parents with all sorts of sweets and chocolates. As he was very generous with it, he became very popular. One day, while we were playing outdoors, he let down his pants and started peeing all over the place. He laughed hilariously and announced, "I am watering the flowers." When he was finished and before pulling up his pants, he walked over to me and said, "Touch it," and then more urgently, "Touch it." I stared in dismay, shuddered and walked away. We were both six years old.

One thing that was lacking in our upbringing was what we now call "sex education." Being one of three girls, I was for an unbelievably long time in the dark about the anatomy of boys, as I had only seen them bundled up in baby carriages or fully clothed. One day I cautiously approached my mother and said: "Wouldn't it be funny if for some time you thought you had a baby girl and later it turned out to be a boy?" My somewhat Victorian mother's expression was annoyed and embarrassed and, being herself too inhibited to use my silly remark as an opening for an anatomy lesson, she only answered, "But, Marianne, don't you know that boys are built quite differently?" I was perplexed. *Built* differently? Yes, boys had bonier arms and legs, wore pants, and girls had long hair and wore skirts, but what else?

Above our washstand there was a little picture of two naked children, shown from the back, entitled "Adam and Eve." One trailed a flowered straw hat on a pink ribbon — that had to be Eve; yet somehow I suspected there must be some difference up in front, and I had to find out. So when nobody was around I furtively took the picture off the wall and turned it over. Frustration! All I found was a piece of cardboard holding the picture in place.

Visits to the Alte Pinakotek and the old Art Gallery on Köningsplatz, seeing the beautiful paintings by Raphael and Rembrandt of the Madonna holding her naked baby Jesus, did nothing to enlighten me on the subject.

Chapter 5

MUSICAL BEGINNINGS

Years before I started learning to play the violin, there were frequent evenings of chamber music in our house. Since children's early bedtime was strictly enforced, I was not allowed to stay up and listen. However, I remember sneaking out of bed and shivering in the corridor to listen to their, I now think, quite amateurish endeavors.

Shortly before my ninth birthday I was told, "You will get something nobody else in the family has." What could it be? The greatest thing I could wish for was a bicycle, but my fa-

ther had one. It turned out to be a half-size violin, the smallest available at that time.

I was neither thrilled nor disappointed. I
had never even remotely thought of playing the
violin. Little did I know then that this small object would become my destiny, would govern the
remainder of my life. Later, as a violin teacher
in America, I learned that some children here,
especially boys, were ashamed to be seen carry-
ing a violin case because the violin was considered a "sissy" instrument. Yet I remember how
proud I had been to carry mine — like a badge of
honor. I never let anybody else touch it.

Because my hands were too small and my
arms too short, I had to wait another six months
to begin lessons. My first teacher was quite
strict, and before every approaching lesson I
hoped she would be sick. Her verdict after a
month was, "Whatever I show her she'll do." She
soon moved away to Berlin. Next came a kind
young lady who guided me nicely through some
of the basics. Daily practicing was routine, just

something you did like brushing your teeth or doing your homework. There was no question of whether you liked to or not. I later impressed this duty, using the same words, upon my pupils, with positive or sometimes doubtful results. Both of my early teachers were actually somewhat mediocre, and my aptitude for the difficult technique of violin playing was not overwhelming, so progress was not particularly rapid.

I was fortunate to have a very musical mother who was able to accompany me at the piano from my earliest lessons on. Over the next few years we played all the Mozart, Beethoven, Bach, and Brahms sonatas together many times over, until one day she declared, "Now I would like ten new Beethoven sonatas." How did we play? I think that by today's standards, probably not too well, but it was like healthy food, good for you no matter how it was cooked.

Around the age of 15 I was still quite shy and inhibited as the following story will illustrate. I was invited to visit an aunt who had a beautiful house and huge garden in Landshut, where I was to meet my second cousin Lilli Palmer (formerly Peiser) from Berlin. We were of the same age and quickly warmed to each other. During our conversation she asked me what I wanted to do with my life.

"I want to be a musician. And you?"

"I want to become an actress," she replied. "But don't tell anyone. People only laugh when I say that."

Eventually, of course, she did become a famous actress in plays, films, and, after the war, in German television. She later married Rex Harrison, the noted English actor.

At one point Lilli said, "You have to come to Berlin sometime — as a matter of fact, I like you very much." I was awed. I liked her too, but for her to say this outright struck me as so sophisticated that I was at a loss for words. I felt like a clumsy Bavarian peasant girl compared to a worldly Berliner. Naturally, I was impressed.

In school I had a classmate whom I especially liked, but who had paid little attention to me. One day I suddenly summoned up my courage and, using Lilli's words, said to her, "You should come to tea some afternoon, as in fact I like you very much." But out of my mouth the words sounded unnatural. When two people say the same thing, it doesn't necessarily come out the same. The girl just stared at me, turned and walked away.

Overall, I was lucky with my school friends, one of whom I am still in touch with across the miles. But of her, later. Another one I must mention, because through her I received my first glimpse of modern art, was Gretl Rupé. Her father was curator of the National Museum in Munich who counted among his friends Furtwängler, Rainer Maria Rilke, Bruno Walter, and others. I will never forget when I visited Gretl in their elegant apartment in Widenmayerstrasse opposite the Isar River. She took me to a room where a large abstract painting covered

most of a wall: it was a Kandinsky. Having
never seen anything but classical art, I was
stunned and deeply impressed by the intensity
of the beautiful yellows and blues and the painting's fantastic forms. I later heard that during
the war the family sold the painting and lived on
the proceeds.

Adolescence is often fraught with problems for young people but for me it was one of
the happiest times of my life. From the diminu-
tive "Flöhle" I had grown — though not much —
and developed in all the right places. My deli-
cate complexion, prone to sunburn, was teas-
ingly compared by a friend to a "kinder popo"
(child's fanny).

I can almost pinpoint the beginning of my
intellectual life. When I was around fifteen years
old I became close friends with three intellectu-
ally outstanding boys, all number one in their
school. They were not boyfriends in the usual
connotation of the word, but soulmates with
similar outlooks and tastes in literature, art, and

music. With Harold I played violin–piano sonatas; with Heinz I went skiing; and with Ernst I went to museums and received private lectures on art.

By far my most significant and long–lasting relationship was with my second cousin, Ernst Kitzinger. We enjoyed reading together — I read aloud, he listened — and we walked along the hilly roads by the Starnbergersee where his family had a country house. It was at that time I began reading Thomas Mann's *Buddenbrooks*, about which Ernst and I had a long conversation.

We went to concerts together, we walked in the Englischen Garten or in the country, and solved all the great problems of the world — or tried to. It didn't seem to matter that he was at least a foot taller than I as we went arm in arm on our long walks, talking and talking. We had the same tastes in literature, enjoying the books of Thomas Mann, Herman Hesse, and Rainer Maria Rilke in particular. It was a warm, sweet intellectual relationship that much enriched my adolescence.

In 1930 when I was vacationing at Tegernsee, he came to visit me. There were other visitors around, so to be by ourselves we rented a rowboat and went for a ride on the lake. The sun was shining, the water was calm except for a breeze, which caused silver ripples to form on the blue surface; and between strokes with the oars we let the boat drift along. A sailboat passed us, the people aboard waving and smiling at us, and we waved back. The whole world around us was smiling. To me it was the most romantic scene I could ever imagine.

This closeness continued until the turmoil of the early Hitler years tore us apart; and though a fairly steady correspondence tried to bridge the gap, the paradise of those teenage years was lost. Political circumstances and the war brought long separations during which we led our own lives and rarely met. Years later Ernst married an English Quaker woman and became a famous figure in his field of art history, Kingsley Porter professor at Harvard University, and writer of many important books on medieval and Byzantine art. I found my life's partner in Fritz Wallenberg, who, you may remember from an earlier chapter, was the student playing in the band at the park, while I played ball there as a child.

During my years of "awakening" I did not follow political events closely, at least not on a daily basis. But I was deeply convinced that whatever was bad was temporary, that everything had to get better. Of course I had no conception whatsoever how this was going to happen; still, I remained optimistic.

There is nostalgia involved with looking back at the time when the world was wider, when big problems were solvable and the outlook for the future positive. It hasn't turned out that way: the world has shrunk, the problems are a thousand times bigger, and at times the future seems bleak.

Chapter 6

MUSIC AND THE CONSERVATORY

To a large extent my musical tastes were formed by having had the good fortune to hear many great performers like Mischa Elman, Nathan Milstein, Bronislav Huberman, Fritz Kreisler and the legendary Jascha Heifetz before they became superstars. It was the golden era of violinists and Munich brought them all. I missed very few concerts, usually getting in with standing room tickets. It became a game to spot empty seats to sit in after intermissions. Every year at Easter I attended the Bach *St. Matthew Passion.* Once, when I got to the box office late, it was sold out. It was impossible that I should miss this concert, so I furtively slipped a Deutschmark into the usher's hand and got in, feeling almost like a criminal.

The concerts I attended instilled in me a deep love and understanding of music. Hearing the Schubert *String Quintet in C major* for the first time, I was so overcome with emotion I had to walk home alone. I couldn't talk because I was sobbing all the way — it was as though lightning had struck. Since then, I have played the Schubert Quintet many times, never without getting a lump in my throat at certain passages. Having composed it two months before he died, Schubert — it is said — had premonitions of his own death when he wrote the trio of the minuet.

At age 15, I declared to my mother, "Music is the most beautiful thing in the world and that's all I want to do." She beamed at my announcement and of course had no objection. Though I knew I would eventually have to earn a living, and abhorred the idea of getting married just to escape this, the risks involved in becoming a professional musician simply never mattered to me.

At my high school graduation, when I was 16, I got my first chance to play a solo with an orchestra – our high school orchestra. I chose the beautiful Adagio of Mozart's *A major Concerto*, which I loved, and for the performance my teacher lent me her Guarnerius violin. Because the stage of the high school auditorium was full of props for a play, the orchestra had to play below it. With no podium available, I had to climb on a table to be seen. Playing on intimate occasions such as Christmas, family birthdays at home, or student recitals always caused me terrible anxiety; but this time stage fright, the dues often paid even by seasoned professionals, was absent. I was able to project my feelings and the beauty of Mozart's music to the audience. It always pleased me immensely when people would tell me my playing had moved them to tears. "It's the music," I would modestly say; but privately I was proud that I was able to touch them.

In 1929 I entered conservatory, the "Münchner Staatliche Akademie der Tonkunst." Standards then were not nearly so high as they are everywhere now, and I did not have much competition. Hours and hours of practicing were meant for prodigies or youngsters with exceptional talent and I was not one of them. My first teacher, Felix Berber, was an ex–concertmaster of various big orchestras and famous locally for his string quartet. Tall, with a shock of white hair and blazing black eyes, he was an imposing figure and I adored him. He was demanding and could be rough at times. I would not have dared to come to a lesson unprepared. But five months after I had started lessons with him, he died of the same strep infection that had taken my father away six months earlier. I was heartbroken.

My next teacher, Professor Kilian, was a kindly gentleman. I think he was an American and very anti-Nazi. He would let loose about the

Nazis, and his wife would hush him: "Careful, careful ..." He was, however, far too gentle a teacher for me at a time when I needed strict discipline. He would give me reproaches, such as "Child, you are lazy," which he spoke with a benevolent half-smile, unable to show the rough hand which I deserved and needed. He was right, but I drew no consequences from his mildly expressed admonition. It did nothing to deter me from spending time in idle daydreams while walking or bicycling through the Englischen Garten to the Poschingerstrasse, where Thomas Mann lived in a stately villa across the Iser River. Mann was my literary hero and I always tried to catch a glimpse of him but never succeeded. My mother was also a fervent admirer of his. She and I would have a contest to see who would be first to read his latest novel as soon as it appeared.

Thus my four years at the conservatory passed pleasantly, perhaps too pleasantly. Taken altogether, they contributed much to my inner growth, but not enough to my development as a violinist. I graduated near the top of my class in 1933, about one month after Hitler came to power. Graduation ceremonies became somewhat of a nightmare in my memory. The student orchestra was conducted by Sigmund von Hausegger, conductor of one of Munich's two major orchestras and director of the conservatory. At the end of the program, a questionable authority from the Nazi party requested that the "Horst Wessel Lied," a Nazi youth hymn, be played. Hausegger refused, laid down his baton and stepped off the podium. Whereupon Karl Blessinger, professor of music theory, jumped upon the podium, grabbed the baton and shouted, "This is the time to be German, German above all," and had the orchestra stand up to play the tune which everybody knew by heart. I wish I had had the courage to walk out at that moment. As it was, I just stood there resting my bow motionless on the strings, tears rolling down my cheeks.

Chapter 7

PARIS

My future lay hazy before me, so it was decided that I should go abroad for further study. In hindsight I know I should have gone to Berlin to study with Carl Flesch, a world-renowned pedagogue; but I had heard him once in a recital that left me entirely cold. Besides, I was in awe of Berlin — the arrogant manner of the people there, their Prussian way of talking and acting. Paris, therefore, became my destination.

Quite alone I arrived at the Gare St. Lazare without any idea where I would turn next. I believe it was a travel agent who found me a place — a small lodging house at Rue du Dr. Heulen, near Montmartre, where I rented a tiny room and had my midday meals. I made breakfast on a small heating plate, and for supper I had soup or whatnot. I was astonished to find the walk to my boarding house quite safe late at night; I was never accosted by anyone — until I realized that on my way I passed a red light district where scantily dressed women sat or stood in doorways, paying of course no attention to me or any other female passers-by.

Beginning my search for a teacher, I found out that the Paris Conservatoire did not admit foreign students. I was convinced that Jacques Thibaud, the reigning French violinist, would not accept me; besides, private lessons with him or his assistant, Madame Astruc, would have been beyond my means. So I was directed to the École Normale at Boulevard Malherbes, a short walk from where I lived, and assigned to an elderly teacher, Monsieur Hayôt, who gave class lessons to about five or six students. I don't think he was a particularly good teacher; I learned more from my classmates than from him.

He paid hardly any attention to me, until one day Thibaud came as a kind of supervisor to listen to each student. After I played the first page of the Mendelssohn Concerto, Thibaud spoke some very encouraging words to me, then conferred with M. Hayôt, seemingly pointing me out as a talent deserving of his attention. After that, things during my lessons turned for the better; and when I helped out in his newly organized student quartet with a viola part, he declared me a "*bonne musicienne.*"

In Paris I was introduced to a completely different culture. Although I did not actually study its history or architecture, and only to a limited extent the language, I let it all wash over me. I was overwhelmed by this city with its unbelievable beauty, its silvery atmosphere, its magic. I strolled the streets of Montmartre and Montparnasse, and stood motionless at the

Place de la Concorde, so awestruck by the architectural proportions that I became dizzy.

At the Quartier Latin, in the student quarters, I saw for the first time a mixture of colored races, chiefly East Indians and Africans. The men walked arm in arm with their female white fellow students, openly kissing without restraint in the subways and on the streets.

At the Ecole Normale there were only French music students among my classmates, and I did not form even a casual friendship with any of them. Not once in the nine months I was there was I invited to a French home, even though one of my classmates, Antoine, took quite a shine to me.

With my plain German clothes, low–heeled shoes, and simple hairstyle, I felt like an ugly duckling compared to the chic Parisians. Generally speaking, it was not a very happy time for me although certain concerts I heard, a visit from my mother, and letters from friends provided some comfort to my loneliness. It was

1934, and at my lodging and elsewhere I was asked, *Qu'est–ce qu'il fait, votre Monsieur Hitler?* — to which I could only answer that he wasn't *my* Hitler. I really wasn't aware of what was then going on in Germany.

During my mother's visit we went to a play at the Grand Guignol, a theater which featured suspense dramas. The play was at least as scary as any Hitchcock movie and left both of us sleepless that night. We had been very close, my mother and I, sharing the same taste in music, books, and art. It wasn't until a few years later that I would loosen our strong inner bond by the kind of rebellion that teenagers act out when trying to find their own identity. In Paris, though, my mother was still a great companion to me, and I'll always remember the day we went to visit Chartres Cathedral, walking arm in arm in animated conversation from the train station towards the cathedral. As we turned the last corner we stopped in mid–sentence. There it was — Chartres, that precious jewel of French treasures, with its magnificent stained glass windows. We walked in and around it for hours, although we did not attempt to climb the 372 steps up to the tower.

My ten months in Paris ended with a rather bad experience. I had met a man, a German, quite a bit older, who professed to be a medical student or doctor's assistant. We went out together, and after four or five encounters, during which we had nothing but casual, general talks, he sat me down at a park bench and seemed very agitated. He handed me two slips of paper: one had a written "yes," the other a "no." This, he explained, was a marriage proposal, and I was to put one of the two slips as my answer into his coat pocket. The whole thing was so absurd that I didn't know what to do or say. I could hardly believe that he was serious, and started to laugh. He became very angry and began threatening me, and I feared that I had some sort of maniac before me. I tried to smooth things over, saying that all this needed much more time and I could not give him any answer. After this I vowed never to see him again. But phone calls came, and when I did not answer, letters came, full of threats. Terrified, I moved out of my lodgings to a friend's place. I knew that he was scheduled to leave for Germany around this time, which was 1934, and I wondered whether he was connected with the Nazi Party. In the end, I never saw him again, but I was so unnerved that wherever I happened to be I imagined I saw him, looming in the distance.

Back in Munich, I remained somewhat in limbo. At home for a year with my mother, I tried to establish myself in the music profession, but my originally accepted membership in the Reichsmusikkammer, the equivalent of a trade union for musicians, was revoked because of my Jewish background. Thus, any professional activity for me was out of the question. My parents had been assimilated into German culture, and were actually registered as *Freireligiose* —

without religion — after my father had signed a certificate that excluded us from the Jewish community. With my relative ignorance of Jewish matters, Hitler's rise to power came as a horrific shock.

Early on in the Hitler years, my oddly "Aryan" looks led to a peculiar incident. I was riding on a train when a uniformed SS man who sat across the aisle started to flirt with me. I am sure I blushed — a curse that followed me even into adulthood — which probably gave off the wrong signal. On descending from the train, he stopped me and, after a few compliments, asked me for a date. I told him that he had the wrong idea, that I was Jewish. Obviously startled, he said, "I don't believe you." When I asked, "Why would I say that?" he answered, "You might be testing me." Aha, I thought, Nazi tactics! I quickly ended the conversation and left.

The specter of Nazism confronted me again in 1934, when something similar happened with my closest friend, Maja. Our friendship had begun during our final years in school, when we decided to exchange violin lessons for gymnastic lessons. Maja was tall, blond, well built, and headed for a dancing career. Soon our lessons became talking sessions — we would meet and confide in each other the most intimate details of our lives. There were times when we saw each other daily, and for a while she became the most important person in my life. She needed me and leaned on me, perhaps more than I needed her, for I was stronger, more balanced, and I gladly accepted the role of being needed. Then one day something upsetting occurred that I can never forget. I can still see the place where it happened. While riding our bikes in the Leopoldstrasse in Munich, we wanted to know what time it was. The only person around happened to be a good-looking young man in a slick SS uniform. Maja approached him with the outstretched arm of the "Heil Hitler" greeting. It felt like a stab in my heart.

I was deeply shocked and I reproached her, but she justified it lightly by saying that at this time it was "the thing to do." It occurred to me that I should break off our friendship right then, but I couldn't. Here it was again: "*Le coeur a ses raisons que la raison ne connaît point.*" Did I lose my integrity by letting my heart rule over my conscience? I don't know.

We still saw each other during my days in Italy, where she came to visit me, and at her home in Weinheim, Germany, where she married her cousin in early 1938. In fact, I played in a string quartet at her wedding. All communication with Germany ceased during the war years, and when it was resumed I did not try to get in touch with Maja. It was she who through great effort later traced me to the U. S., beginning her letter, "Finally I found you."

The same soul–searching I had done in the Leopoldstrasse began again: Should I respond and renew our old ties? I knew that her husband had fought in Hitler's army, that they had to be

members of "The Party" to survive (whether will-
ingly or not I did not know). When later on I
questioned her, "Didn't you know about the concentration camps, about the annihilation of the
Jews?" her answer was, "We heard about it, but
we just didn't believe it."

I asked myself for the umpteenth time:
What would I, what would we have done if we
weren't Jewish? I don't know. Maja and I saw
each other again during my first trip back to
Europe in '47 and have seen each other many
times since, keeping up a regular correspondence in between.

Chapter 8

ITALY

As luck would have it, through my aunt's previous visit to Italy I was offered an *au pair* job with an Italian family in Varese near Milan for the summer of 1935. I was to give violin and German lessons to the 14-year-old son of a middle-aged couple. Sandrino, the boy, was a nice and talented lad, but lazy, and the whole thing turned out to be more a vacation than a job. Some close relatives of the Reggioris, my Italian family in Varese, often came over for visits from Milan and promised some help, should I settle there. I knew I would have to leave Germany before long, and this seemed as good a place as any. From the very beginning, I took to it like a duck to water. During my first evening at the Piazza della Scala I said, "I think I'll like it here." I had a modest room on the fourth floor, from which I could see the Monte Rosa. I loved the gentle climate, the lively temperament of the people, and the beautiful language that I quickly learned and came to speak fluently.

I would be remiss if I did not mention another attraction — a handsome young man named Dino, the youngest son of the Reggiori family in Milan. He had black hair, blue eyes, a high forehead, and a classic Roman profile. In the course of time, we became passionately involved, but our paths were star-crossed from the beginning. Not long after I had installed myself in a furnished room in Via Vela near the Viale Abruzzi, Dino was called into the army to serve in the Abyssinian War. My appeal for his exemption to Senatore Cappa, to whose home I had been frequently invited, proved futile. His first question was "Does he belong to the Fascist party?" I shook my head. To my satisfaction, the whole Reggiori family was anti-Fascist. The senator sighed and shrugged, "If you swim against the stream, you can't expect to land safely."

And so Dino was shipped to Abyssinia for a dreary eighteen months. During that time I became comfortably established in what I thought was to be my adoptive country. I lived modestly in a furnished room, with meals cooked by the landlady. She gave me a lot of pasta, and only when she served uccellini — tiny birds considered to be a delicacy — did I go on strike. She laughed, "You eat chicken, don't you?" True, but eating little songbirds seemed barbaric to me.

Making friends, mostly with fellow German refugees, came easily, in sharp contrast to my Paris days. I assembled a few violin students, gave a recital in Varese once, played lots of chamber music and also played in a private chamber orchestra, L'Orchestra d'Archi di Via

Paolo Andreani 6, at the home of Avocato Ansbacher, a prominent Milan lawyer. Ansbacher
was a friend of Toscanini's, and once had engaged Adolf Busch, the great German violinist,
as soloist. The orchestra was conducted by Paul
Kletzki who became well-known as both a composer and conductor in France and England. After each session at Ansbacher's we were served
sumptuous refreshments. They were not the
main reason I was there, but I must admit they
were part of the attraction. Of course, there was
daily practicing, the harness into which any serious musician is forever strapped.

Though I was not endowed with great
technical facility, what carried me through, I
think, was innate musicianship, a nice vibrato
and tone, and an ability to project my love of
music, particularly in the classical string quartet
literature, my greatest joy.

All that time I was anxiously waiting for
Dino's return. When he finally came back in late
'38, it took us a while to find our way to each

other again. But then, unexpectedly, the Italian government decreed that all foreign Jews were to be expelled from the country. Although Italy was not basically anti–Semitic like Germany, Russia, Poland, and to some degree many other countries, Mussolini had caved in to Hitler, making a deal to obtain coal from Germany in exchange for adopting anti–Semitic measures in Italy. My three happy years ended as I was forced once again out of a country that I loved. With a heavy heart and an unknown future before me, I left Italy in February 1939, and went to England to join my family and wait for an immigration visa to America.

Chapter 9

LONDON

Despite dire warnings from all sides, my mother had remained in Munich out of loyalty to her 80-year-old mother-in-law, who could not be moved, and partly because she didn't realize the ever more dangerous situation for Jews. When dear Granny mercifully died in late 1938, my mother left for London, narrowly escaping the horrors that took place in Germany shortly afterwards. In London she was welcomed by her two older sisters, and also by her own daughters who had gone there to pursue their studies: Edith as a doctor, and Irene as a psychiatric social worker.

England required a work permit for non-citizens, and in order to protect its own, would not give me a work permit as a musician. All I could have done in London was to be a "domestic," a maid in a rich English household, and that did not appeal to me.

Those were dismal months in London. The damp climate, cloudy skies, and reserved people were in such sharp contrast to Italy's sparkling atmosphere, to which I had responded so spontaneously, I became rather depressed.

True, there were pleasant moments, such as visits with my second cousin, Ernst Kitzinger, who with hundreds of others was later deported to Australia as an "enemy alien." (England did not treat its German refugees much better than America its Japanese residents on the West Coast.) I spent six weeks in Cambridge keeping a music professor's wife company during his intermittent absences. And as I did everywhere I ever lived, I played chamber music. When air-raid sirens warned of German bombings at the beginning of the London Blitz, we drowned them out with late Beethoven quartets.

The best moment during all that time came when Dino, on the pretext of a business trip, arrived to see me in late August 1939. After a few glorious days together, fate struck its third blow. With Hitler's declaration of war imminent, Dino caught the last plane back to Italy. Finis. My visa to immigrate to America, for which I had applied as soon as I had to leave Italy, came in the mail. I had waited for a year and a half, and I left within the month.

Chapter 10

IMMIGRATION

The scariest moment in my life occurred in October 1940, during my passage to America. The day before our ship, the Samaria, departed from Plymouth, the children's transport ship, the Benares, had been torpedoed by German submarines. It had been headed towards the U.S. and was evacuating British children from the Blitz, which had begun to devastate the British Isles. After our ship was two days out to sea, I was lying on my bed coping with a bad case of seasickness when there was a loud rattling from the hull of the ship, followed by the ominous alarm that commanded everybody to their lifeboat stations. I barely dragged myself to the designated station, flopped flat on my back on deck, and thought, "Thank God, the boat goes down." Even today I get seasick when I see a picture of a boat.

The boat did not go down, and five and a half days later we landed safely in New York Harbor. By then I had fully recovered and along with everyone else on the boat, I raced to the side that was passing by the Statue of Liberty. I had seen pictures of the great lady, but she seemed bigger and more impressive up close. This symbol of welcome was all I encountered on my arrival; a friend who was supposed to meet me did not show up and could not be reached by phone. I felt totally lost.

Since all my immigration papers were in order there was no question of my being sent to Ellis Island, at that time a dreaded place of detention for irregular immigrants without visas. As it was getting late in the evening, a kindly captain let me sleep another night in my cabin.

The next morning I got in touch with an old friend, who promptly picked me up and settled me in a furnished room on the upper West Side.

The day after settling down in my rented room, I went out for groceries. Although it was the middle of the week and not a national holiday that I was aware of, all the stores in the neighborhood were closed. Then I found out it was Yom Kippur; I was amazed that this was reason enough for so many stores to close.

My mother had transferred a small sum of money to a New York bank for me to dip into as I needed it, so I was never really in want. But after drawing $50 from what I always considered *her* account, I decided I must begin to make it on my own. I had met a relative of the family who told me she had a job as a waitress. It dismayed me to hear this because in Europe it would have meant sinking into what was considered the lower class, a drop not easy to climb up from.

Though my parents had always treated our servants as equals, it was unthinkable that the cook would be anything but a cook. But here you could be a waitress or a salesgirl or anything, and still be a lady. How wonderful...What a free country! I began to scan the newspaper's classified columns and under "Help Wanted" found an ad that said, "Waitress, experienced, daily 12-2, Wall Street district." I didn't pay much attention to the word "experienced"; — after all, how can you gain experience without doing it?

Just two hours suited me fine, and I applied. When asked where I worked before, I mumbled "Buffalo," hoping they would never follow that up. The place was a horseshoe–shaped lunch counter, and all I had to do was relay the orders through a window into the kitchen. Simple. But when the orders came: "Tuna on whole wheat with lettuce and tomato, easy on the mayo," and next: "Two eggs once over lightly with ketchup on rye toast," I, having never heard of whole wheat, ketchup, etc., got utterly con-fused.

My complete downfall came when one cus-tomer asked for a pickle. I called through the kitchen window, "She wants a pickle." The fel-low behind the kitchen window said, "Get one of them little plates." On the counter there was a stack of thick three–inch bowls, and although my English was generally quite fluent, I did not know what a pickle was. Thinking it was a nick-name for those little bowls, I placed one before the customer, empty. She and her friends started to giggle — it was obvious they thought I was a half–wit. When closing time came and I asked "Tomorrow, same time?" the chef sadly shook his head. "But I thought this was a steady job?" With obvious pity in his eyes, he said, "No, honey, it was only as a substitute." Of course, he had found me totally inadequate — which I was.

And so, rather downcast, I went home thinking, "So I can't even be a waitress." But there in the mail was a letter from Thomas Mann (cf. Appendices). It was a handwritten answer to a fan letter I had written to him after reading his *Lotte in Weimar*. Without even taking my coat off I sat down, opened the envelope and started reading. "You have written me a very charming, touching letter," he began. Instantly, my waitress experience was forgotten, and I felt like a princess in disguise. Years later I received another Thomas Mann letter, again in answer to mine with my enthusiastic comments on his *Josef's Legende*, and this one has been published in one of the printed volumes of his letters — my remote claim to a touch of immortality.

After the fiasco of my waitress job, I again skimmed the "Help Wanted" ads in *The New York Times*. I skipped all the waitress ones and found one that said, "Wanted: Messenger girl, no experience necessary." I thought I couldn't go wrong with that and went to the given address.

The office turned out to be a windowless cubbyhole in midtown, large enough for only a desk and chair. The rather sullen-looking man behind the desk handed me a huge pack of envelopes and explained that all I had to do was deliver them on the eleven floors in the two buildings across the street. It was the garment district in Manhattan and the envelopes contained the bills for the merchants. With the minimum wage being thirty-five cents an hour, this was a cheaper way of distribution than the two cents postage for each letter. "Easy," I thought, and set out on the assignment, not counting on certain physical conditions that were involved in it.

I was not used to stifling New York summer days with temperatures in the 90s and equally high humidity. I entered one of the high buildings with its old, hand-operated elevators that the operator had to bring level to each exit floor. Every floor he lined up meant jerking the elevator up and down before he opened the clanging gates. Since early childhood I have always had a motion–queasy stomach and could not even enjoy the swings and carousels in rec-reation parks. So, before disaster struck I had to get out to the fire escape for some fresh air. Finding the exit, I sat down for about ten min-utes on the platform of the fire escape. Then, unable to trust myself on another elevator ride, I thought I could do the job using the fire escape from floor to floor. But the fire doors were locked from the outside. Since I simply could not face another elevator ride, there was nothing to do but wend my way down about ten floors by the iron stairs and return to the office with half the pile of letters undelivered. Feeling sheepish, I said, "I can't do it. I get sick on the elevator." Af-ter he gave me a disgusted look, I added, "You don't have to pay me." He didn't.

Chapter 11

MUSIC IN NEW YORK CITY

My first rooming house offered no kitchen privileges and, of course, I could not afford to eat out. Even Horn & Hardart's, that fascinating cafeteria where coin–operated, glassed–in display counters offered all kinds of appetizing food for a few nickels and dimes, was way beyond my modest budget. My search for a place to live was always dependent on one condition: that I could play the violin as often as I wished.

After several weeks, I found through an ad in *The New York Times* a beautiful studio on Riverside Drive with a spectacular view of the

Hudson River and George Washington Bridge. My room rent with kitchen privileges was $6 a week. My landlady was Mrs. Weisskopf, an elderly woman who let me cook my meals, and also practice my violin as much as I wanted. Often at 6 p.m. in her somewhat croaking voice she would call from the kitchen, "Miss Lissmann, will you have a bite with me?" Since I was living on $50 a month, all expenses included, this was a godsend, and I gladly accepted. But our conversation moved along quite primitive lines. She was from the South, and only gradually did I find out what that could mean. It was an eye-opener on America when she began to talk about "those colored people" (whom she obviously despised) and which she elaborated on by her prejudicial phrase, "God made them black to do the dirty work." My appetite soon waned in her company, and I decided to make my own meals.

There were no supermarkets at that time, only butchers and bakers and greengrocers. I was astonished by the large quantities that people bought, and when I said to the butcher, "I want a pork chop," he grimly asked, "How many?" When I timidly answered, "Just one," he practically threw it at me. It cost only nine cents.

My first, quite meager earnings came from giving weekly violin lessons to a middle-aged man who came to my place. I had found him through a musical agency created to help refugees. His desire to play the violin was considerably greater than his ability to do so, but I didn't mind, as I loved to teach. Lessons were once a week, until Mrs. Weisskopf put an end to it, declaring the arrangement wasn't proper. "What would my neighbors say if they saw a man walk right into your bedroom?"

No such complications arose with the next pupil, an amateur whom I taught at his own place. It never even crossed my mind that going alone to his modest apartment — a railroad flat on the upper West Side — could be in any way awkward or even dangerous. He was about 50, a perfect gentleman, obviously single, and had a fair musical background.

In England I had learned that it was bad manners to ask about a person's occupation, and I had no idea where he worked. He never volunteered any information, and he was only free after 4 p.m. and on legal holidays. Always well-dressed, he seemed well-educated and I wondered what he could be — a worker, perhaps, in a bank, an office, a law firm? I couldn't guess. After about twelve months, curiosity prevailed and I asked him what his profession was. I still can't get over the shock I felt when I saw him blush to the roots of his gray hair. "I'm a school teacher," he mumbled.

A teacher! Where I came from teachers were called "Herr Professor" and looked up to with the utmost respect. To me theirs was the noblest profession; yet this poor man felt ashamed to be a teacher. It was then I found out that schoolteachers in America were on the lowest professional pay scale, grossly underpaid and sometimes inadequately educated. Fortunately, this has radically changed since the early '40s, though not enough, considering the importance of teaching for future generations. Teaching — the desire to share what I'm able to do and enjoy — was a natural inclination for me. Respect for learning, either for myself or others, emerged early and prompted my classmates to often say mockingly, "*Ja, Fräulein Lehrerin*" (Yes, teacher).

One of my most dedicated students was a girl named Denise, who had to have a full body cast after a scoliosis operation. Knowing that the cast would be on for many months, she insisted on having part of the cast cut out next to her left shoulder, so she could hold and play her violin.

Strangely enough, after seventy years of teaching, I don't miss doing it now. Three years ago I was diagnosed with an affliction called macular degeneration. It prevents me from reading music and has put a halt to my playing and teaching. Yet I am happy knowing that many of my former students play in various community orchestras, or play in quartets for enjoyment. Five or six of them, now graduate students or mothers, play in our local symphony.

Even though California had been the destination on my original ticket from England, by 1941 I had more or less given up the idea to move there. The music markets and auditions for jobs for all over the country were at that time mostly in New York City. I soon found a group of chamber music players to perform with, but somewhat later had an awkward encounter with one of my new colleagues. After quartets one day, I got a call from a young girl, who said that she wanted to help me because I was "different" from the other refugees. "How come?" I asked. She hedged — "Well, those other refugees, they push and push..." She was speechless when I said, "But I am Jewish." It had taken me years to say so without blushing. There was silence on the other end of the telephone, and our conversation stopped rather quickly.   Needless to say, I never heard from her again.

It was not until later in 1941 that I became a member of Local 802, the powerful musicians' union headed by the "Czar" Petrillo.   It required a six months residency to enter 802, the equivalent of a "green card" for immigrants engaged in other occupations. As it turned out, my then lack of union membership gave me an opportunity to play on stage at Carnegie Hall, in a small group led by a Mr. Durieux. It was a benefit concert with Gertrude Lawrence and the composer, Percy Grainger, as the principal participants. I should have been awed to be on stage "in these hallowed halls" ("In diesen Heil'gen Hallen" from Mozart's *The Magic Flute*), but I was too new in New York to know what Carnegie Hall meant.   I have since heard many wonderful concerts in this Hall that Isaac Stern saved from demolition in 1960.

Chapter 12

CAMP LENORE

A job in Massachusetts tided me over nicely in the hot summer of 1941: I became a counselor in a girls' camp in the Berkshires, seven miles from Tanglewood. In Germany, Italy and England, summer camps were fairly unknown, so this was an entirely new experience for me. Camp Lenore was all Jewish, although not labeled as such. Their only bow to religion was a brief service every Saturday morning conducted by Mr. Spectorsky, the camp's director and owner. (Camp Lenore, still in existence, was written up in a feature article a few years ago by Diana Trilling in *The New Yorker*).

It was an easy job, and all my expenses were paid. My duties were to bunk with four six–year–olds, see that they brushed their teeth morning and night, tuck them in bed, and get them up in time for breakfast. I was amazed at the quantity of food served — daily platters of meat and butter that would have added up to at least a week's rations in wartime England. Yet some of the children, obviously spoiled, complained about it being "too starchy," that variety was lacking — this was hard for me to stomach.

Besides having learned some English in school, I had picked up a fairly complete knowledge of the language in the eighteen months I lived in England with my family, waiting for my American entry visa. I was unaware that my English differed in pronunciation from American English. Naturally, I spoke it with a British accent, which greatly amused the children in camp. They made fun of it by imitating me: "I saw the caaalf go down the paaath to take a baaath in a minute and a haaalf."

In addition to my counseling duties, I played violin in a piano trio at almost every Saturday morning service. We played parts of the Arensky trio, plus bits of other trios, all put together by Mr. Spectorsky. The other trio members were a cellist from Berlin, a refugee like myself, and Ruth Antine, a pianist-composer from Brooklyn, who had studied with Hindemith at Yale and who became a lifelong friend. One of the most positive thinking people I have ever known, she can make you see a rosebush where there is only a mud hill.

As the camp was near Lenox, we three often hitchhiked to Tanglewood and sat on the lawn outside the shed, listening to the concerts. Our own trio performances led to a concert once in New Haven. Calling ourselves the "Berkshire Piano Trio," we gave a benefit performance for the Russian war relief. Our program was the

Mendelssohn *Piano Trio in D minor* and a solo piece for each of us.

The morning after one of our performances at the camp for the staff and older children, a youngster stopped me on the way to my cabin and said, "You played very nicely last night. When did you give your first concert — if you ever gave one?"

Amused, I answered, "Well, perhaps at 18, when I played in a semi–public recital."

"Oh," she said, a little contemptuously, "My uncle gave his first concert when he was nine." Seeing how eager she was to talk about her obscure "Uncle," I asked, "What has become of him since, does he play in an orchestra?"

"No," she said ... "he travels ... He is a soloist ... He is Jascha Heifetz."

I jumped about three feet in the air. Sure enough, it was little Ann Chotzinoff, the niece of the man considered the greatest violinist ever.

Chapter 13

TOURING

After I became a member of Local 802, my union card meant I could apply for any job in music. My first big opportunity came in 1942 — a U.S.O. tour halfway around the country with a group of five girl violinists, a pianist and a singer, booked to entertain servicemen in Army and Navy camps.

This job, however, came at a price: because of it I missed a chance to play quartets with Albert Einstein. I had heard all the jokes musicians told about him when he missed a cue, ("Albert, can't you count?") But I also heard that he played "relatively" well, and I was eager to play quartets with such a famous man. A chamber music friend of mine, Immanuel Velikowsky, whose controversial book, *Worlds in Collision*, is still talked about in scientific circles, was a friend of Einstein's, and arranged for me to play quartets in Einstein's Princeton home. Unexpectedly, our tour manager had scheduled an audition for his show the very same afternoon. I stammered something about having a previous commitment, but the group leader said, "If you want to lose this job, go ahead with your previous commitment." Later, I learned that this was just a scare tactic. But because I couldn't afford to lose the U.S.O. job, I asked a friend to substitute for me at Princeton. I have regretted ever since that I gave up the chance to play quartets with Einstein.

For the U.S.O. tour I was to audition for a Mr. T., who was assembling the group. This Mr. T. was a small man with blinking eyes, a thin mustache and a heavy Russian accent. He told me to play anything I wanted, so I played the piece I always used for auditions, the *Preludium & Allegro* by Kreisler. It is very effective when well-played and sounds more difficult than it is. I must have worn a tight sweater that day, for while I was playing his gaze never rose much above my chin. After I aswered the obligatory questions — was I in the union, was I willing to travel — I was accepted for the tour. The pay was $50 a week, of which I expected to save about half. Our lodgings, even though they were in third class hotels, were always clean, and a decent meal in nearby restaurants cost under a dollar.

The first performance of our show was to be held in a Washington, D.C. theatre. As we approached the city in our company bus, traffic was getting more and more congested and we realized we would never make it in time for the performance. Our driver tried weaving in and out of traffic to speed us along when suddenly a whistling police car pulled up alongside and signaled us to stop. After a brief discussion between our driver and the policeman, we were surprised to find ourselves in the middle of the road behind the police car, its sirens blasting to push cars aside. As all other traffic yielded to make way for us, we grinned, felt very important, and arrived in the nick of time.

Our group was part of a variety show, which also featured a comedian, and two actors who did a skit on army life. We gave three shows a day. Arrangements for our ensemble, plus a harp, included snatches of the Grieg *Piano Concerto* and Jerome Kern's *Smoke Gets in Your Eyes*, always our biggest hit.

One problem with the U.S.O. job was that I wasn't allowed to wear my glasses, which I needed for reading music. We had to be glamorous young girls in flowing blue chiffon gowns, so wearing eyeglasses was out. Contact lens science was in its infancy then: lenses were the size of an eyeball, and intolerable for me to wear for more than an hour at a time. All during the tour I kept my age, 27, a deep dark secret, as the

other girls were much younger than I. They
clung together as children do and made me feel
a bit like an outsider.

This did not bother me too much, as I was
absorbed in gaining fresh impressions of the
new country around me. Everything was im-
mense compared with Germany, France, Italy,
and England. There were miles and miles of
fields without a house in sight, and vast
stretches of woodland except for an occasional
farm with peculiar round–domed grain elevators.
The people also were different — men were very
tall, women often stout, children quite loud and
unrestrained.

Our group traveled mostly by bus, but occasionally by train. The tour, after dozens of
stops at Army and Navy camps, took us through
the Eastern states to the deep South, and it was
there that I learned even more about discrimination in the United States. I had only a superfi-
cial knowledge of American history, slavery and
Abraham Lincoln, and was shocked to encounter

the ongoing aftermath. During twenty years in Germany I had never seen any blacks, and in Paris I saw them treated as equals. Yet, in the American south at train stations the toilets were marked "White" and "Black," signs in restaurants said "Whites only," and even our own train wagons were all white. One day, to show I disapproved of all that and demonstrate my solidarity with the "colored" people, as they were then called, I went into the "Black" compartment and sat down. I saw only a lone black woman. Obviously not understanding my intentions, she stared at me with such hate and fury I was afraid she was going to spit at me, perhaps attack me, and I fled. A few days after this I was walking in a small town in Alabama when a black woman approached from the opposite direction. As we came closer, she stepped off the sidewalk until I passed. I wanted to say to her, "Don't, there is room for both of us" — but by then I had given up my crusade for civil rights.

I learned first hand a great deal about America on that tour. The other girls would say "I'm Russian," or "I'm Norwegian," etc. — even though none of them had ever been far beyond Brooklyn. I began to realize everybody came from somewhere else, at least one or two generations ago. My roommate was Lillian Anderson, the "Swedish" one, and the singer of the group. She was a beautiful tall blonde with a pug nose and sweet baby face. She chose me as a roommate because I didn't smoke and all the other girls did. Not surprisingly, she was often asked out by G.I.'s from our audience, and I went to bed alone and a little envious.

The Army and Navy camps were mostly located around small towns, so it was my first chance to get a glimpse of small–town America. Between shows I had ample opportunity to stroll around. What struck me most in comparison with the European countries I had lived in was that all the smaller houses were made of wooden shingles (aluminum siding was still practically unknown). Flimsy, I thought, when compared with all the stone and brick buildings I had known abroad. In Germany, fences; in England, hedges; and in Italy, walls had marked divisions between properties. Here there were driveways with garages at the end. All open, with none of the privacy I was used to. I thought that if ever I should land in a place like this, it would be the end of the world for me. As a matter of fact, I have lived in just such a town for the last fifty–one years, and it has by no means been the end of the world.

Having graduated from the Staatliche Akademie der Tonkunst (the Munich conservatory) with A's in violin performance, and with a few public appearances under my belt, I came to the U.S. with, I'm afraid, an overblown opinion of myself. "What do these Americans know about music?" I thought. My balloon was soon pricked and shriveled when I heard Juilliard students play rings around me; so I resolved to take lessons.

With the money I saved from the U.S.O. tour, I sought out Rafael Bronstein, a Russian violinist, who was the father of seventeen-year-old Ariane Bronn (her artist name later on), the soloist in our show number. Rafael Bronstein was a pupil of the legendary Russian teacher, Leopold Auer, who taught Heifetz and Milstein, among others of past generations. Another of Bronstein's pupils is the world-famous Elmar Oliveira.

Ariane's solid technique convinced me her father was the best teacher for me and I began lessons right after the U.S.O. tour ended. Knowing my precarious financial situation, Bronstein charged me only five dollars a lesson — a lesson that lasted at least two hours and often included lunch with the family. During one lesson when I was working on the Bruch *G minor Concerto*, he said, "Marianne, you have someding dat should be heard by de pipple." I felt flattered, realizing that I must have succeeded in projecting my deepest feeling for the music. Yet I knew I lacked mastery of the excruciatingly difficult technique that the violin demands and was far from even aiming at being a concert soloist. Besides, I had to make a living.

Bronstein kept me informed of available orchestra positions and where auditions for them would be held. At that time knowledge of such events — which took place only in New York City — was conveyed by word of mouth. Nowadays, orchestras must advertise their vacancies through the Musicians Union paper. There is a refundable application fee and auditions are held at the orchestra's home base. Although this involves considerable expense for the applicant, there are great numbers of people auditioning — usually from 100 to 200 — for the violin sections of major orchestras. In my day there were no more than ten or twelve musicians trying out for an orchestra job and my chances were infinitely better than they would be now.

I decided to audition for the New Orleans Symphony. After I finished playing, the manager and the conductor spoke in Italian in front of me. They were talking about how much they would pay me in order to make my salary lower than the average, so they could fill another post as well. They didn't know I was fluent in Italian and understood every word they said. Of course, I turned the job offer down.

Since the U.S.O. tour I had begun to acquire a taste for touring, and found it relaxing to travel and play at the same time. Everything was taken care of. A written itinerary told us where we were to go, which hotel we were booked into, which theater we were to perform at and what time we had to be there. Have your luggage outside the door at a certain time. Meet the bus, which takes you to the train in an hour. Evening performance at 8 p.m. All that remained was to enter the theater and play — usually the same repertoire. Life on the road was easy — too easy, and I admit that it didn't do my violin playing much good. But the job that I landed in 1942, a cross-country tour with the "Ballet

Russe de Monte Carlo," paid one hundred dollars a week, a princely sum that enabled me to pay back every penny my mother had deposited for my start in America. I felt rich. For the first time in my life I could open a savings account and pay taxes.

However, this tour, which took us only to good-sized cities, proved to be both musically and personally unrewarding. At that time Alexandra Danilova was the reigning Prima Ballerina, and Maria Tallchief, who eventually rose to the top, was a promising youngster. Danilova insisted on calling me Susi — "I'm not Susi, I'm Marianne," I would say, but she never seemed to hear me. Usually we had our own special train. The dancers seemed to be obsessed with their feet, resting them across their seats onto adjacent ones, which forced the rest of us to stand up in the aisle. Many dancers on the train played poker with the blinds pulled down. As we were nearing the "Royal Gorge" in Colorado, I wanted to open the shade in my compartment

and look out, but they wouldn't allow this because the blinding sun would upset their poker
game. "But we are passing under the Royal
Gorge!" I cried. "Oh, we have seen it before," they
said.

In their view and that of the audience, we
were only orchestra musicians, way beneath
them in status, almost their servants. I am sure
that except for the top ballerinas the dancers
were poorly paid, but as I found out, they had
an interesting if not quite legal way to save
money on lodgings. One of them would check
into the hotel as a single, go to the room —
which always had double beds — come back
down and whisper the room number to an unregistered friend in the next ascending elevator:
thus two for the price of one. It was called
"ghosting," the unregistered roommate being the
"ghost."

There were only three girls in the twenty-
piece orchestra — a cellist, a violist, and myself –
– and I chose to room alone. One day the other

two girls had a falling out, and the cellist suggested she room with me. She wanted it the ille-
gal way, and mostly out of curiosity, I agreed.
She was an unusual girl, half East Indian and in
many ways quite interesting. The day before our
venture into ghosting she had missed the company train, but caught up with us by bus. Our
"ghosting" worked beautifully until the next
morning, when a strange thing happened.

While at the bathroom sink I had taken
off my ring, an heirloom with small diamonds
and sapphires. At breakfast I remembered that I
forgot to put it back on and raced back to the
room, but it was gone. I couldn't report it to the
desk because I wasn't registered — I was, after
all, only the "ghost." I searched all over, explaining to my roommate that I had several times
mislaid or thought the ring lost, but that it had
always come back to me. She said, "Have you
looked in the wastepaper basket — you must
always look in the wastepaper basket." I
thought her suggestion an odd one but did what

she said. There, tightly wrapped in a bus ticket, was my ring. I stared at her, mystified, but she only said, "Hurry up now, we're late!" and dashed out the door.

I never found out what had been on her mind when she did what she did. If she had wanted to steal the ring, she could easily have hidden it among her belongings. Why did she crumple it up in her own used bus ticket and at the last minute speak those peculiar words about looking in the wastepaper basket? Was it when I told her that no matter how often I had thought the ring lost it had always come back, that had moved her? During the long tour I had always enjoyed sitting and talking with her, but thereafter I never roomed with her again. Nor did I attempt any more "ghosting."

After my first cross-country tour with the ballet ended, I heard of an opening in the Pittsburgh Symphony. The conductor was the famous and much feared Fritz Reiner, and I decided to try my luck with him. Somehow, just

a couple of days before the audition, I had gotten
wind of the pieces he always gave the applicants
to "sight–read." One was the very difficult first
page of Strauss' *Don Juan*, and the second, certain pages from Wagner's *Tannhäuser*. I prac-
ticed feverishly day and night. After I "sight-
read" the *Don Juan* rather well, Reiner, known
as a holy terror at rehearsals, smiled benevo-
lently and said, "You have played this before,
haven't you." I said, "Yes," and when he asked
where, I stuttered, "In ... in London." Then he
put the Tannhäuser in front of me and I said,
"This one, though, I have never played." I did
well with that, too, after which he said, "We have
just accepted a woman — so if we don't find a
man who plays as well as you, we will take you."
That was in 1943 when very few women played
in orchestras: Today he certainly would not have
gotten away with that kind of discrimination.
Not surprisingly, I did not get the job.

My next audition turned out very differently. It was for Leopold Stokowski and his

short-lived "New York City Symphony Orchestra." After I played my solo piece, he had me sight–read a page from a first violin orchestra part that was unknown to me. Although sight-reading was never a strong point with me, I did well enough.

Stokowski then asked me who I thought the composer was of what I had just played. I guessed Brahms. It was Tchaikovsky. He then asked, "Do you think Brahms should be offended and Tchaikovsky be flattered by your guess?" I nodded and could see he was quite amused. I was immediately accepted in the second violin section and started my first regular symphony orchestra job.

The most embarrassing situation I'd ever been in occurred during one of the rehearsals. Stokowski interrupted the playing, stared at me and called out to the manager: "Mr. Vanni, could we have a little table with some coffee for the inside player at the third desk — she looks so very comfortable and relaxed the way she sits with her legs crossed." Having short legs, I almost always sit cross–legged, but did not know that this was absolutely taboo in orchestra playing. It was my first day playing in a professional orchestra, and there I was, an object of hilarity for my colleagues. I blushed a dark crimson and wanted the earth to swallow me up. Seeing my embarrassment, Stokowski quickly went on with the rehearsal. Never again did I cross my legs while playing in an orchestra or any other ensemble.

Playing under Stokowski's direction — I will not say under his baton because he did not use one — was a remarkable experience. His hands were extremely expressive, and when he conducted Wagner's *Liebestod*, they became almost erotic. No bowings were marked in our music. I had always seen the string section of the great orchestras bow uniformly, whereas Stokowski's peculiar speciality was arbitrary bowing — in fact, when you happened to use up or down bows in unison with your desk partner he'd call out, "Change it."

After playing with his orchestra for a few weeks, I met Stokowski by chance in the hall of the auditorium. He caught my adoring glance and stopped me briefly to say, "You are doing very well," which more than pleased me. However, I couldn't help taking it as an apology for having embarrassed me at the rehearsal that day.

New York in the forties was a very pleasant and safe place to live. It was even safe to ride the subway home alone at 1 a.m. after a concert. At this time I lived in the Village at 123 West 10th Street — in a small two-story townhouse that had a skylight. Even though it was boiling hot in the summer directly under the roof, and freezing cold in the winter with inadequate heating, I never dreamed of looking for different quarters because, with an absentee landlady, I could practice as much as I wanted, often a problem when looking for places to live. Like my first studio apartment, the rent was $6 a week, including cooking privileges.

Sometimes, after I'd returned from tours, the noise outside my window made by the trucks travelling towards the West Manhattan harbors would wake me up at 4 a.m. But I quickly got used to it and, after a week back in the city, blissfully slept through it.

In mid-season I was offered the chance to play in Adolf Busch's chamber orchestra, a new ensemble that was scheduled for a cross-country tour. Surprisingly, I had no trouble breaking my contract with Stokowski's City Symphony, as there were many waiting to fill my position. Adolf Busch was then probably the only great German violinist of his generation. His gift was profound musicianship more than virtuosity; his reper-toire, confined to the classics — Bach, Beetho-ven, Mozart, and Brahms. Early on he teamed up with the young Rudolf Serkin — later his son-in-law — and performed the whole classical sonata literature. With his younger brother, a cellist, Goesta Andreasson as second violinist, and the violist, Paul Doktor, he founded the famous Busch Quartet.

As a person he oozed charm, and his audiences, including myself, worshipped him. With his tall, burly figure, round head, blond hair and blue eyes, he was the archetypal German. After banning all Jewish musicians, the Nazis would have dearly loved to prize him as their own. He would have had the field to himself, but his unwavering integrity and sterling character did not allow him to remain in Germany. As early as 1933 he immigrated to Basel, Switzerland. Because this territory was too proximate to Germany, there were rumors of a possible kidnapping. So he moved to America and settled in New York. There, where virtuosity and technical perfection such as Jascha Heifetz personified were valued above all, he did not quite regain the stature that the musical climate in Europe had given him.

In Europe the high wave of the audience's admiration carried him over such technical hurdles as are strewn into the Brahms Concerto; but here in America there were no established adoring crowds. As a result, orchestra engagements became fewer, and this probably prompted him to form his own group, the "Busch Little Symphony." When in December 1941 I heard that he was assembling a chamber orchestra for a cross–country concert tour under Columbia Concerts Management (besides Hurok, the most prestigious in the East), I did not hesitate to audition. Busch had always been one of my heroes and I found the opportunity to be on his musical team irresistible.

For my audition, held in his New York apartment, I played the Brahms Concerto. He corrected just about every phrase and fingering, and I was sure I had failed. Then he said, "Yes, I'll take you." I was thrilled. "I will put you in the second violins." That was fine with me as long as I was *in*. After three or four rehearsals — to my surprise and delight — he moved me into the first violin section.

I had always enjoyed touring, but of all my tours, this one was the most memorable. The members of the group were pleasant and congenial, and every concert an event. At each performance Busch himself would play a solo violin concerto; and while we were in the East, Rudolf Serkin sometimes performed with us. We had our own bus and driver, making stops mostly in big cities across the country.

For some reason we played not one but two concerts in Reno, Nevada. At that time it was extremely difficult in the U.S. to obtain a divorce, and Nevada was the only state which granted one after a six weeks' residence. We were lodged in two different hotels there, and mine was the one not on the itinerary. I went to the other one in the morning after the first concert and asked if I had any mail. There was none, and the clerk offered to subsequently for-

ward it to me at the other hotel. "No, thank you,"
I said, "I'll be back tomorrow morning."

"But lady," he said, "it will be very incon-
venient for you to come here every morning for
six weeks."

I laughed and said, "I'm not even married,
and I'm moving on soon, anyway."

He probably thought the only reason I was
there was to establish the six weeks' residence
necessary for a divorce. He gave me an embarrassed smile and apologized.

Between the last two Busch tours, I was
engaged as a counselor for the Cape Cod Music
Center in East Brewster. The camp belonged to a
Mr. and Mrs. Crocker, who were staunch Repub-
licans. Not knowing much about American poli-
tics, I was surprised when my admiring remarks
about President Roosevelt made Mrs. Crocker
seem ready to scratch my eyes out.

Each of the counselors gave a recital. At
one of them, given by Irene Beamer, the singing
teacher, I heard for the first time Mahler's *Songs*

of a Wayfarer, which became one of my favorite Mahler compositions. For my own recital I played the prelude of Bach's *E major Sonata* and the Bruch *Concerto in G minor*.

One of the more outstanding campers was Lillian Kallir, a beautiful 16-year-old with two long dark braids, who later became a famous pianist and also the wife of the pianist, Claude Frank, and mother of the acclaimed violinist, Pamela Frank. Years later Ms. Kallir appeared as one of the first soloists with our orchestra in Binghamton.

One day while at the Music Center, I received an unexpected letter from Fritz Wallenberg asking me to join him and a few of his friends, who were vacationing in New Hampshire.

Chapter 14

MARRIAGE

When I was quite young, I often dreamed of marrying an architect who was also a musician. With Fritz Wallenberg I came close. Fritz was born in Danzig, then a German city, now Polish Gdansk. He was brought up in a musical family; his father, by profession an ophthalmologist, was deeply involved in the music of J. S. Bach and gave lectures on the composer at his home, with himself at the piano. His mother was a singer, but being the mother of four she was not on the stage.

Fritz's instrument was the cello; however, as so often happens with people gifted in music, he wanted to be a conductor. His father, aware of the difficulties a musical career held then, as it does now, advised him to learn a practical profession first. "After that you can do what you like."

So what were his choices? Medicine was out because, like his two younger brothers, he was red–green color-blind. When you can't see blood, or if a face is pale, you cannot be a doctor. Law did not interest him; however, as he liked tinkering with things he chose engineering. Endowed with talent in both, he studied music and engineering simultaneously in Danzig, Berlin and Munich.

Immediately upon receiving his technical diploma he turned to music, holding posts as conductor in Schwerin, Neisse, and, briefly, one in Holland. After Nazism terminated all that, he immigrated to Colombia, South America. Ultimately he landed in New York, and spent his first year as a cellist in the Indianapolis Symphony. He soon grew restless with orchestra playing, but as he had no connections, he found conducting jobs were as remote as stars in heaven. By 1942, when American war preparations had begun in earnest, he fell back on his second profession, and even without any experience quickly obtained a job as a designer in a small engineering firm. When the firm closed, he found work with Agfa Ansco, the big photographic chemical firm, which had an office in New York.

Fritz and I met playing string quartets at the house of a mutual friend in 1944. With my frequent touring and long absences from New York, we saw each other only intermittently. We played quartets for several years before we played duets, during which our mutual admiration turned into love.

We were married in a civil ceremony at the municipal courthouse in New York on April 25, 1947. An amusing prelude came just before this momentous occasion: The day of the wedding Fritz picked me up at my place, gallantly holding a bunch of red roses, and we unceremoniously took the subway down to the courthouse. Fritz's sister, Lotte, and her husband were the only relatives around to be our witnesses, and as they prepared to meet us in front of the courthouse, I suddenly remembered that I had left the required marriage license at home. Quickly thrusting the flowers into Fritz's hands, I said, "I'll get it — I can do it faster alone," and turned on my heels. I will never forget the horrified expression on my future sister-in-law's face when I looked back at the next corner. I'm sure she thought I had panicked, changed my mind at the last minute, and run away. After a half-hour delay, though, all went smoothly and we were man and wife.

Our similar backgrounds and love of music, in addition to our mutual desire for children, brought us to a beautiful life. Enrichment came through our shared music and Fritz's support of all my musical activity. Without his encouragement I might have given up my violin when the children were born.

Wherever we went on vacations (except abroad), our instruments went with us, neither of us willing to spend more than a few days without practicing. Even on our honeymoon to Connecticut in our newly acquired Chevy, the violin and cello came along, having their honeymoon in the trunk.

Chapter 15

BINGHAMTON

When Ansco's New York office closed in early 1947, everybody was dismissed except Fritz, who was given the opportunity to transfer to their headquarters in Binghamton, New York. He accepted, and thus we began our married life in the "provinces." As a newly licensed driver Fritz found the drive from New York to Binghamton to be such a strain that we interrupted our trip and stayed overnight in the little town of Callicoon.

Having spent my earlier years in Munich, Paris, Milan, London, and New York, I was rather apprehensive about moving to an un-

known small town like Binghamton. The area
had a college, known as Harpur, which previously had been an affiliate of Syracuse University, and was still housed in military prefabs in
nearby Endicott. A few years later it moved to a
large campus in the adjacent Town of Vestal
where, with Governor Rockefeller's generous
help, it became by 1965 one of the most prestigious universities in the SUNY system.

Old Route 17 was not the same as it is
now and had not yet been properly paved. As we
approached the Susquehanna valley all I saw
were rising smokestacks belonging to the area's
three most prominent industries — the Endicott
Johnson shoe factory, General Electric, and
IBM. What reconciled me from the start,
though, was the beauty of the city's surrounding
hills and its stretches of green fields. That first
year before our daughter was born, we often
drove to the outskirts of town, where we found
many pleasant country roads to walk on.

The postwar housing shortage was still acute in 1947, and accommodations in Binghamton were hard to find. Fritz wanted to be within walking distance of his workplace, Ansco, where he was designer supervisor in the engineering department. Our first living quarters, an unfurnished apartment we rented on Chapin Street, contained for a few months only our beds, a card table for dining, and a grand piano.

My mother had owned twin Blüthner grand pianos, and right away she let us have one of them. When after a few years it accumulated too much mileage and Mother had stopped playing, she sent us the other one. The piano had been battered during the Blitz in London when an incendiary bomb hit her house (fortunately nobody was at home), and had been restrung and refurbished in Cambridge. It was then crated and shipped, addressed simply to "Wallenberg, New York, N.Y." Miraculously, it arrived at our house.

We had to leave the Chapin Street apartment after two years because the other tenants complained that we made too much noise. Really, one could not blame them. I would practice the violin in the morning; Fritz, after dinner and nap, played his cello and piano; then together we played violin–piano sonatas. This would happen in any apartment, of course; so the only solution was to buy a house. Because we'd lived only in big cities we had no idea how one went about buying a house. We knew nothing about mortgages or down payments, assuming we had to pay the whole sum at once — like buying a loaf of bread or a pound of apples.

Worse yet, at that moment a so–called efficiency commission was visiting Ansco, and they soon began firing people in all departments. When Fritz explained our present dilemma of buying a house to his chief engineer, John St. John, the chief assured him that Fritz would be the last one to be let go in their department. The very next day the chief engineer was fired. As a pure coincidence, Fritz had the score of Bach's *St. Matthew Passion* on the piano at the time of this crisis and one day I had turned the page to where Jesus says, "One of you will betray me," and the apostles all ask, "Is it I?"

Is it I? Is it I? This was how we felt from day to day about the firings; everyone was trembling and wondering: "Who will be fired next?" As it turned out, Fritz was not fired, and we finally found an affordable little brown shingle house on Binghamton's West Side, within walking distance of Ansco. That it was also within easy walking distance of primary and middle schools was of no consideration for us then, but later on proved quite a boon.

The West Side location must have formerly been a German settlement — the streets around us were called Schiller, Goethe, Beethoven, Mozart, Haendel, and Haydn. Once, an alert youngster who came to audition for lessons with me looked around our bookshelves and spotted the Beethoven biography by H. C. Robbins Landon:

"Oh, Beethoven," he exclaimed, "that's like the street!" Our house was at 2 Bellevue Heights, cornering Schubert Street. We would have liked to reverse our entrance door to make ours a musical address, but that wasn't practical.

Close by was Recreation Park, a small park with swings and slides and a big carousel. Like all the other carousels in the city's parks, it was given by George F. Johnson, founder of the Endicott Johnson Shoe Company, with free rides for all. As a boy he had lacked the nickel it cost for a ride. Having never forgotten this, he vowed that nobody should be denied a ride on his carousels for lack of money. I found this a typical example of American generosity. I often took our daughter Kathy to Recreation Park, and when she was two years old she said, "Want go on the lala," her name for the music-playing merry-go-round. Even though I was prone to motion sickness, I bravely took her for a ride. She was happy as a lark, while my ordeal began. Not only did the carousel move ever so swiftly, the horse on which we sat holding tightly moved up and down, adding to my discomfort. When it finally stopped, we got off, Kathy squealing with delight, I white as a sheet. I had to sit down on a bench to recover, and decided then and there that in the future only baby sitters would take her on carousel rides.

The house we bought had belonged to an old couple who obviously hadn't done the least bit of upkeep. We had to put in a good deal more money to make it livable, and after replacing the coal furnace with a gas heater and modernizing the kitchen and bathroom, we enclosed the upstairs porch to give us a spare room. It took years to get the coal dust out of a basement cubicle, which became a convenient storage space. All this extensive remodeling has made it a comfortable home for these last fifty years.

The large front porch was also enclosed and transformed into living space, enabling us to fulfill one of Fritz's long–standing ambitions — to perform Bach Cantatas in one's home as his father had done. Although Fritz had featured several of Bach's two hundred surviving cantatas with the orchestra in public, his bimonthly performances of them took place in the intimate setting of our home. We had a small chorus, a miniature orchestra consisting of a string quartet, double bass, and whatever wind player and vocal soloist the score required. Before each cantata, Fritz would illuminate the music and the text with a few words. My role was to play first violin and afterwards to put refreshments on the table. Fortunately, I had help, especially from our friend, Ethel Molessa, who recruited the singers, cleared performance dates and organized a group of strong men to put away chairs. These Bach evenings went on for several years after Fritz's retirement from the symphony, and are one of the many accomplishments he looks back on with pride and satisfaction.

Being active as he was in two professions — engineering and music — made for considerable stress in our daily life, but we managed to

adjust. For me, too, it was a demanding schedule, particularly after our dream had come true
with the birth of our two children — Kathy and
Jim.

On August 22, 1948 our daughter Katherine Louise was born. After all had been taken
care of in the labor room, the nurse placed me
on a gurney and put the tiny infant between my
bent, outspread knees. We were taken into an
elevator to go to my third floor room. They
pushed the "up" button and closed the door. At
that unforgettable moment, I truly thought I was
going to heaven.

On April 26, 1952, our son James Theodor
was born. The experience of *giving birth* — how
beautiful these two words are in the English
language. We were a quartet now, although a
different kind from the ones Fritz and I had
played in New York. Though much had happened to me, both before and after, I would say
that these two events were the most fulfilling in
my life. Now, fifty years later and with waning

strength, I wonder how I managed it all — children, household, teaching, practicing, performing, and a husband who needed his share of my attention — perhaps quite a high wire act. For present-day working mothers, with husbands pitching in, something Fritz with a double profession could not do, this may not seem to be such a responsibility, but for me, then approaching middle age, it was not so easy. At the time, though, I was unaware how busy I was and took it all in stride.

When Jimmy was a child we had warned him to be careful with strangers, because they could be wicked and harm him. But he took my lesson a bit too far. Once we had some friends bring a friend of theirs over, and Jimmy suddenly said to the unknown person, "You are wicked." The poor lady asked why. "Because you are a stranger," he said.

I very much wanted to do the right thing with the children, instill values and set goals, and I could only do so by applying what life had taught me, what my instinct told me and not least what Dr. Spock said — then the bible for new parents. Fritz to this day pooh-poohs Spockism, calling it "Scheissology." As an engineer, Fritz puts more stock in concrete principles and proven ideals.

Chapter 16

THE SYMPHONY

My mother came for the birth of both our children. When she arrived for a visit in 1955, I said to her, "You came when Kathy was born. You came when Jimmy was born." My mother's face fell — she thought I was pregnant again. Then I added, "And now you come for the birth of a symphony." The symphony was our third child.

Our first chance to do some musical pioneering began with the help of Isidore Friedland, director of the Jewish Community Center. Izzi was a genuine music lover, a kindly man with a voice so highpitched that when he answered the phone, people would impatiently repeat they wanted *Mr.* Friedland. He quickly recognized Fritz's potential as a conductor, and under his center's sponsorship, with the unwieldy name of "Jewish Community Center Chamber Orchestra," we began our public musical life. We had assembled some 20 players, mostly music teachers and a few amateurs, and played our first concert at the Monday Afternoon Club to a "small but appreciative audience." Fritz gave me the opportunity to solo with the orchestra — Bach's *Concerto in E major*, plus Beethoven's *Romance in G*, op. 40 as an encore.

Still coexisting with our group was the "Triple Cities Symphony," which had limped along with an out–of–town conductor, and, after a lingering death, finally came to a halt. The obvious thing was for this organization and ours to merge, with Fritz at the helm. The nucleus of the now defunct T.C.S. soon merged with the Jewish Community Center Orchestra, and we called it the "Community Symphony." However, at about the same time a new opera company had sprung up, and its conductor, Peyton Hibbitt, also wanted a hand in conducting a new symphony orchestra. There was a tug of war between his loyal followers and ours until, on an impulse, I called up our local newspaper and told them to print that "Fritz Wallenberg was the new conductor of the symphony." A friend to whom I later told the story called it "chutzpah." It probably was; but it worked. Nobody questioned it, nobody asked "Who says, how come?" and the battle was over. But the real battle had just begun.

Binghamton at the time was more or less a musical desert. As an example: when I called the only music store in downtown to inquire whether they had the Haydn Trios, I was met with silence. When I repeated "Haydn Trios," the answer came — "Is that the name of the song?" For many years the only choral group in town, the "Choral Society," had alternated exclusively between performing Handel's *Messiah* and Men-

delssohn's *Elijah.* When Fritz took over the chorus's leadership, this was radically changed as
he plunged the group into an abundance of classical choral music hitherto unknown in the area.

How does one launch a symphony? The
Jewish Community Center had given us $250
for expenses like advertising, hall rental, and the
printing of programs and tickets. My own
knowledge of organization and fund–raising was
zero, but I knew that industries subsidized some
artistic endeavors. Local headquarters of the gi-
ant IBM were in Endicott, and I felt we had to
approach them. I made an appointment with
the general manager to plead our case. To my
surprise, he graciously received me — a nobody
— and assured me they had a budget for such
things, but that it had to be matched by the
community. He offered the royal sum of $250,
which meant we could forego the sponsorship of
the Jewish Community Center. This gave us a
leg to stand on, although fragile. But what now?

I was told that to begin with we had to have a board. What's a board? All I knew was an ironing board or a cutting board for the kitchen. All right, first get a president, vice president, secretary, and treasurer. With the help of our close friends, Morris and Debbie Gitlitz, a prominent lawyer and his wife, a staff was soon recruited. Our good friend, Harry Lincoln, flutist and professor at Harpur College, also came to the rescue. He agreed to accept the position as head of our newly founded symphony, and in fact was president of the symphony twice. At our first concert Fritz introduced him — "Ladies and gentlemen, you won't believe it: I present to you, President Lincoln!" Laughter, and right at the start the ice was broken.

We soon established a board of directors and a subscription series, but still many organizational details rested on our shoulders. Fritz laid out the programs for the printer, which we had to proofread after tiring Wednesday rehearsals so they could be ready by the weekend concert. Several of us carried our posters to libraries and shops, wherever they could be displayed. None of the players were paid, so rehearsal attendance was accordingly spotty. A missing key player like a first trumpet or second clarinet would provoke a wild stare at me from Fritz, the poor frustrated conductor. "Where is Dario?" and I, equally frustrated, had to put my fiddle down and make a telephone call, only to find the missing player at home. His excuse: "I couldn't make it."

When we started our chamber orchestra there was no local oboist around. I love the oboe and always had a hankering to learn to play it. There is a general belief that oboe players are a bit strange, perhaps because of the pressure exerted on the brain from blowing through the narrow reed. Fritz was not in favor of my taking up the oboe and said jokingly, "You are crazy enough as is." But the main obstacle was getting an instrument, as they were very costly. Then somebody told us of a man whose wife had an oboe. I eagerly asked, "What about her, doesn't she play anymore?" He shook his head, "No, she is in the State Hospital." That was the end of my oboe ambition.

Gradually our budget grew, with other businesses besides IBM and more individuals from the community contributing as sponsors and patrons. We could now begin to pay baby sitter money and transportation expenses, and, of course, pay our name soloists. Concert agencies had regular, special, and very special fees for their artists. For us, of course, they requested the very special fees. During the first years it was for many of our local musicians, and certainly for Fritz, a labor of love. In time a volunteer manager was added, and eventually the musicians unionized. The union helped to the point where musicians came on time, did not simply stay away without an excuse or, as sometimes happened, wordlessly leave at intermission. As standards rose, our friend Morris Gitlitz, a member of the violin section from the

beginning, decided it was time for him to quit,
doing so gracefully with the quip, "An orchestra
which accepts me as a player isn't good enough
for me."

  We played two symphonic, one Pops, and
two choral concerts a season, all at Binghamton's West Junior High School and later at the
downtown Forum. How fortunate we were to
play and the community to hear the wealth of
classical music Fritz programmed — such gems
as Haydn's *Creation*, Bach's *St. Matthew Passion*, the Verdi *Requiem* for the Choral Society;
and for the orchestra alone, symphonies by Beethoven, Brahms, Dvorak, Schubert, and Mahler.
Soloists like Leonard Rose, Garrick Ohlsson,
Szymon Goldberg, Lillian Kallir and others,
graced our concerts.

  As assistant concertmaster I usually un-
derstudied the violin solos at rehearsals; then
one day Fritz offered me the chance to perform
the Bruch *G minor Concerto*. Being a little un-
sure of myself, I took the concerto to a lesson

with the famous teacher, Ivan Galamian, in New York. After hearing me he asked, "You plan on playing this with the orchestra?" I shrugged, then he said, "It'll go, it'll go." That was it: Galamian had said so — so I accepted Fritz's offer to schedule me. After much agony, anxiety, and many nightmares, it did "go," I think even quite well.

A résumé of our programs sent to Harold Schonberg, then the top music critic of *The New York Times*, prompted the following reply: "I have looked over the programs with a great deal of interest. They are superb and would do credit to any musical organization in any major city of the world. Congratulations on the good work you people have been doing!"

Eventually the rich store of works for smaller ensembles led to the formation of the "Symphonette," with a nucleus of about twenty symphony players, and conducted by Fritz. For a musician like him, of course, conducting is the ultimate gratification. However, for a string player like myself, without the talent or ambition for a solo career, it is playing string quartets. From the time when my mother played piano trios with friends in our home, I have loved chamber music above all else. My greatest joy came later when I myself participated, which I have done wherever I was.

Early on in Binghamton, we were fortunate to find a young couple, Sanford and Joan Reuning, with whom we linked up to form the "Wallenberg Quartet." Joan played viola, Fritz, the cello, and Sanford, a willing second violin. I was the uncontested first, and never ceased to feel privileged to play those glorious first violin parts. These sessions were for me the absolute highlight of my musical life. After we began giving performances, a few interested friends suggested forming a Binghamton Chamber Music Society, another first for the city.

We played two or three public concerts a year for six years. After the Kennedy assassination our quartet was asked to play a short memorial on television, sponsored by Hamlin's Drug Store. I pondered what to play. Immediately, the key of G minor popped into my head, and I felt that Mozart's *G minor String Quintet* would be the most beautiful piece we could do. What is more heartrending than its opening? Adding a second viola player (Melba Sandberg) to our string quartet we played the first two movements and were immediately invited for several more TV appearances. Then, in '63, our partners moved to Ithaca and our quartet came to an end. The timing was good because one year later the newly formed Guarneri Quartet moved into residence at the University. Thus we had gone out in our glory, instead of being "buried" by those superior musicians who soon afterwards became world-famous.

In the '60s a government subsidy called Title 3 allowed us to repeat the orchestra programs in Elmira and other outlying districts. In one of these small towns, a lady was so delighted with our performance that she wanted to engage the orchestra for a gala garden club meeting. Costs were discussed, and it soon became apparent that paying for the orchestra was out of the question.

"Well," we said, "we also have a smaller group, our 'Symphonette,' which would be far less."

"How many are in the Symphonette?" she wanted to know. We told her, "About twenty." Doing some figuring she still found it was too much.

"We also have a string quartet," we said.

"How many are in your string quartet?" she asked — I was tempted to say "the usual five" — but, as it turned out, no concert for the garden club was scheduled.

Of all the nearly 200 orchestra concerts we gave, I missed only two: on April 25, 1952 when Jimmy was born, and on June 19, 1970 when I drove to New York City for Kathy's college graduation.

Fritz retired after twenty-five years at the head of the Symphony. Originally, we had named it the Community Symphony, but as we grew, that name had been changed to the Binghamton Symphony to give it a geographic identity. Recently, after merging with the Pops, it has become the Binghamton Philharmonic.

Chapter 17

VIOLINS

I have played the violin for 76 years — the average life span for women in the U.S. The violin that I played most of my life was given to me by my grandmother, when I was about sixteen. It was my steady companion during my four years at the conservatory in Munich, my studies in Paris, three and a half years in Italy, one and a half years in London, and the rest of the time in the U.S.

The certificate it came with says, "From the school of Petrus Guarnerius," and the label inside, "Petrus Guarnerius, Mantua 1759." However, its authenticity has always been difficult to establish and is a puzzle even to experts. It has been seen by old Bisiach in Italy, who, after inspecting it, exclaimed, "Camillo Camilli," then took a little sponge which he dunked into the bowl holding his cup of glue. To my horrified amazement he used plain warm water to wash off some dirt on the violin's table, whereas I had always used special cleaning oil.

Sacconi, a longtime employee at Wurlitzer, proclaimed, "Yes, it's a Petrus Guarnerius."

Nicogosian said, "No, it's definitely not."

Chris Reuning, who is now set up in an elegant shop in Boston, was as puzzled as others who had seen the instrument, but advised me to show it to Darius d'Attili, a top authority on old violins, who lived in New Jersey. I took it to d'Attili, and after he studied it silently for a long time, he looked up and said,

"You gave me a hard one."

His final verdict was: "It's definitely Italian, definitely about 200 years old, but who made it is almost impossible to say."

As to the price he wouldn't commit himself either, but threw out a figure: "200-year-old Italian starts at about $50,000" — quite an increase over the 2,000 German Marks my grandmother had paid for it in 1929.

I had another experience — typically English — at Hill's in London. Taking my violin along, I went to buy an A–string at the world-famous Hill Store on Bond Street — a store I'd always wanted to see. As old Mr. Hill attended to me, I slyly opened my case. After one glance he snatched up the violin and looked at it from all sides for long minutes. He then put it back in its case without a word. I couldn't help asking, "Do you like it?" "I haven't heard it," was his haughty reply. People with his experience don't have to hear an instrument to know at least approximately what it is.

A real find for me were violins made by Ansaldo Poggi (1893–1984), a violin maker from Bologna. I first heard and played a Poggi violin when one of his instruments changed hands in my house. Soon afterwards I commissioned one directly from him. In an extensive correspondence with him, where my knowledge of Italian came in handy, he admonished me to be patient — "*Bisognio asciugare*" (It has to dry). It took one and a half years for me to finally get the violin.

Poggi would not mail his instruments or accept checks — a violin had to be picked up in person and paid for in cash. Much as I would have liked it, a trip to Italy was not feasible at that time. I was lucky, however, for my English nephew, Peter, had gone to Italy for a medical convention and offered to pick up the violin for me. Arrangements were made. He cautiously notified the English import authorities that he would bring in an Italian violin, but that the instrument was to go to his aunt in America a few weeks later. It would be taken there by his other aunt (my sister Irene), who was scheduled to visit me. They told him this was no problem — they would put the instrument in their air-conditioned storage where they kept various art treasures, and release it when my sister started her trip.

So far so good.

After picking up my violin from Mr. Poggi, Peter was careful never to leave it behind in his hotel room, taking it along on his sightseeing tours. He told me,"Your violin is probably the only one that ever went up the Leaning Tower of Pisa."

Something surprising happened when he returned to England to have it put in storage as previously arranged: As soon as the checker in one of the many lines heard his story, he said, "Aren't you the chap who called us two weeks ago about a violin later to go to your aunt in America? Then take it along — no storage necessary." Of all the control men in those lines, he landed the same one he'd spoken to before leaving!

We nicknamed this violin the "Lady Wallenberg," in imitation of naming famous Strads after their former owners. Shortly afterwards I bought two more Poggis, and in the thirty years since I've owned them their value has increased forty-fold. Not all violins, even modern Italian ones, have appreciated as much, so perhaps my instinct and ear led me in the right direction.

The violin was quite prominent in our son Jim's general education from an early age on. Because Jim was small for his age as a child, I took him to learn some basic karate, so that he'd be better able to defend himself against school bullies. Having heard that karate-trained people could split a brick with their bare hands, I anxiously asked the instructor, Hidy Ochiai, whether the course could affect Jim's hands. He grinned and said, "Make hands like steel." "Thank you," I said, and we quickly turned around and left.

As I am unable to play anymore, the future of my violins now lies literally in my son's hands.

Chapter 18

FINALE

The tape is running out. Among my childhood toys was a kaleidoscope that never ceased to intrigue me. I was fascinated by the beautiful patterns it showed, no matter how you turned it. One day it broke, and I still remember staring in disbelief at the little heap of red and green and yellow chips of glass in various shapes which, lying on the ground, made no sense at all. The prism inside the tube was still intact, and *that* was an optical revelation for me. Through the prism of my brain, I have tried in these pages to assemble all the colorful pieces of my life, hoping they emerge in a pattern that will make some sense.

If it is true that the American dream is a family of four (statistics say two and a half children — although I never could figure out how to have half a child), a house and car, professional fulfillment, earning recognition, having financial security in old age, and good health most of the time, then my husband and I have achieved that dream. Fate has been kind to me: I have two wonderful children whom I'm fortunate to stay close to. Jim, musically gifted and with an outgoing nature, has played in the Toronto Symphony for many years, spicing this up, both informally and in concerts, with a sprinkling of chamber music. His hobby is performing in stand-up comedy using his violin as a prop, à la Jack Benny. Katherine, also gifted and very bright, is a many-sided individual who, after various professional detours, is now a psychotherapist in New York.

I have become ever more aware of the astonishing century I've lived through; it contained probably more earthshaking events than at any other time in history — with two world wars, Hitler's rise and fall, radio and television, the Kennedy assassination, putting a man on the moon, to name only a few. The world changes each day, but I will leave it for others to unravel the mystery of computers, the recent advances of science and technology, and the understanding of avant-garde music.

Many years ago I asked a cowboy who took hotel guests at Lake Louise for rides along the lakeside, "I've never been on a horse before -- can an old lady like me still get on a horse?" He said, "You are not old, lady, you just have lived a long time." By now, I really *have* lived a long time and the "Golden Years" may not always be so golden — they are often quite brassy, instead.

Though various physical problems have crept in gradually over my eight decades, now they become more manifest. Be it the knees, the hips, the ears, eyes or the heart, few people reach this age untouched. Movements are slower, feelings less intense and stamina shorter. One says "Thank you" more often than "You are welcome."

Nobody knows the end. For the future, my greatest wish is that I may not fall burden to anybody, especially my children, and that the end may come gently. No hurry please, but occasionally now Bach's *Cantata No. 82* comes to mind. The text is: "Ich habe genug" — I have had enough.

Ich ha - be ge - nug,____

ACKNOWLEDGEMENTS

My deepest gratitude goes to my friends and editors, Professor Kenneth Lindsay and Christine Lindsay, without whose expert guidance, enthusiastic support and countless hours of work through all the crucial phases of realization, this book would not have come into being.

Many thanks to the Director of Global Publications, Dr. Parviz Morewedge. His ready acceptance, wise counsel, artistic involvement and expertise gave the book its final push and filled me with confidence and joy.

Thanks are also due to John Hyland, who deciphered my hand-written manuscript and put the fragmented pieces into proper order on the typewriter. Further thanks belong to Judith Besanceney, who started the process of editing and patiently put my many afterthoughts where they belonged; and to Jay Datema, who read aloud to me what I had written and put the text into computer form.

Finally, I am grateful to the many friends who encouraged me along the way and urged me to "get on with it."

APPENDICES

- Letters from Thomas Mann

Pacific Palisades, Calif.
740, Amalfi Drive
den 26. IV. 41

Sehr verehrter Fürstin,

Sie haben mir einen sehr ...
..., vergangenen Sonntag geschrieben, ...
... ich sehe mich noch ... jungen geschehen,
... mittelbar Werke ... mal ...
... Lawinia ... ... Um Gote,
... Du brich, halte die Nerven" so
lieben! ... ... unser ...
Körper. So sehr es ... ...
... ... den Gott gestellt. ...
... ... gesundsten Geistes, ..., ...
... Gott spielt, ...
... Gotte Eines — ... ...
... ...

Ich danke Ihnen für ... alles, ...
...

Unsere Haushalt in ... haben wir aufgelöst und wollen den Sommer hier verbringen. ...

Ihr ... ergebener

Thomas Mann

THOMAS MANN

1550 SAN REMO DRIVE
PACIFIC PALISADES, CALIFORNIA

8. Okt. 44

Sehr geehrter [illegible],

mit Ihrem Brief haben Sie mir eine herzliche Freude gemacht. Immer war ich [illegible], den Lesern der deutschen Ausgabe zu gönnen, [illegible] diese Vorausgabe, die [illegible] ohne meine [illegible] hergestellt und die New York photographiert, mit Fehlern, Auslassungen etc. [illegible]. [illegible] ich die deutsche [illegible], [illegible] eigenen [illegible]. Wie [illegible] ich die Absicht, daß sie [illegible] Übersetzung braucht. Man muß sich eine Absicht vorstellen, die auf [illegible], der die [illegible] zu verstehen und zu verstehen, daß ich an den 1800 deutschen Exemplaren in Amerika mehr Freude habe als an den 200000 englischen.

- Family Album

Adolf Dünkelsbühler
(grandfather)
ca. 1910

Julie Dünkelsbühler
(grandmother)
ca. 1910

Josef Lissmann
(grandfather)
ca. 1920

Berta Lissmann
(grandmother)
ca. 1925

Luise Lissmann
(mother)
ca. 1930

Dr. Paul Lissmann
(father)
ca. 1925

Fritz and Marianne

Edith
(sister)

Irene
(sister)

Fritz

Katherine and James
ca. 1954

Katherine and James

The Wallenberg String Quartet

Binghamton Symphony

Binghamton Symphony and Choral Society
April 26, 1969
Binghamton West Junior High School